To Jane Browne and her great staff—Kathy, Jennifer and Matthew—who had the patience to nurture this project through to success.

ANN JUSTICE

Ann Justice is an Appalachian hillbilly who was transplanted to Wisconsin twenty-some years ago. A return to the hobby of weaving gave her the idea; her biking husband gave her the hero; and her concern for displaced persons of all ages gave her the inspiration. In real life, Ann writes . . . at her computer . . . while taking long walks with her dog, Gramps . . . standing in checkout lines . . . working in her garden . . . soaking in a hot tub . . . watching TV . . .

SARA'S FAMILY

Ann Justice

A KISMET™ Romance

METEOR PUBLISHING CORPORATION
Bensalem, Pennsylvania

ONE

Harrison Hixon was having some major problems focusing. His brain refused to stop spinning video replays of the rain, the cold, the dark, the curve that he hadn't seen coming as he pumped his way up the steep mountain road. Suddenly the soft shoulder of the road had given way to a drop. He was falling, the bike went flying, and he hit ground . . . hard, unyielding ground.

That's the last he remembered except for sporadic flashes . . . rain soaking him . . . the silence . . . finally a car or truck backing up . . . voices moving toward him . . . then again the nothingness.

Now as he struggled toward consciousness, his leg hurt, his back hurt, his face hurt. On the other hand he was dry or at least not constantly wet. Had the rain stopped? He tried to focus but blackness was the only thing he saw. He couldn't seem to communicate to his eyelids to open. He felt movement—maybe he was still falling. How steep was the cliff . . . how far the drop? He cried out and reached for a branch, a rock, anything to break the fall.

A child's worried voice: "Is he dead?"

Harrison found that he was inordinately interested in the answer.

"I doubt it, though heaven knows he probably deserves to be." This from a woman. Nice of her to be so damned concerned. "Is he comin' 'round, Ling?"

Ling?

Man . . . Asian accent . . . close by . . . "I think not."

Then the fading murmur of those voices plus others . . . more children . . . all in slowed time and from far away. The motion he hadn't even noticed stopped, doors slammed and he was riding high . . . carried. Hands against and under him. Then softness except for the leg. Hardness down at the leg. His message center was down. He tried to bend his leg—nothing. He tried opening his eyes—nothing. He tried saying something to the voices— nothing. God, what if he had really hurt himself? What if there was real damage . . . brain damage? He closed off the racing thoughts and returned to the blackness.

Later—whether hours or days, he could not have said— Harrison once again struggled to open his eyes. This time he met with at least partial success. The place was dark, though there was enough brightness from outside to make out shadows and shapes. With so much light, there must be a full moon. He wondered if it had stopped raining at last.

Across from where he lay he made out the image of a woman . . . a ghostlike form standing in front of a dresser brushing her hair. *Catherine*. He struggled to come more fully awake, fought to keep his lids open, felt the pain that ripped through his head and leg as he struggled to get to her. *Catherine*.

Impossibly she moved toward him, sat next to him, placed her cool hand on his cheek and forehead. She was touching him and he could feel it. That meant only one thing . . . she was here . . . really here. With a burst of effort he captured her arm and pulled her toward him. He kissed her and, when she struggled to pull away, he held her more firmly, the weakness of his accident leaving him as he concentrated all his energy on having her stay.

"Catherine," he mumbled, his emotions a jumble of relief at her being here and rage for what she had put him through. "Oh, Catherine."

And then his other hand wrapped itself in her hair and he kissed her hard and full on the mouth. He couldn't believe it. Catherine, here. After all this time. But he was holding her, his hand burrowing into the luxurious mane of hair. He was kissing her, his mouth on hers in a hunger he had thought could never be satisfied again.

But, no. It was the dream again . . . she was pulling away. He held tighter, kissed deeper. *Stay*, he pleaded with his hands and mouth. *Please, stay*.

And then he was exhausted. He collapsed against the pillows, wondering for just an instant where he was before he slept again.

It was dawn the first time Harrison fully woke up and looked around. The room was small, rustic. It had the scent of furniture polish and lavender. It was filled with old furniture—some valuable antiques if he was any judge. It was a woman's room . . . probably the woman sleeping in the rocker. Her age and looks were hard to determine since her long dark hair covered her face. She was wearing some sort of chenille bathrobe that looked as if it had seen more than a few washings. She was tall, judging by the way she fit in the rocker.

Where the hell was he? Who was she? And what the devil was he doing in this get-up? He half raised up to catch a better look at the loud tropical yellow and green muumuu he wore and then collapsed with a groan.

Taking a second look, he saw the crude splint by the bed, felt the pain in his leg, and everything came rushing back . . . the storm, the mountain road, dark . . . why the hell didn't these people put in guard rails if they weren't going to light the roads? And then he recalled the sudden downhill curve that had doubled back and flying through the air. . . .

His bike. He glanced around the room. No sign of it. The woman might be tall, but she certainly hadn't been strong enough to get both him and the bike back here . . . wherever here was. It was awfully light out and yet the clock by the bed said five o'clock.

He focused again on his leg. Why the hell didn't she get a doctor? Or take him to an emergency room? What was going on here . . . he'd heard stories . . . hell, he'd seen *Misery*. What had possessed him to venture back into these mountains in the first place?

"Good morning, Harrison Zachery Hixon, Jr." She was awake and up at once, bustling around the room, pouring water into a glass and offering it to him. "You must be thirsty . . . not to mention hungry."

He could have sworn she blushed at the word hungry, but then in the bright light he couldn't really tell. She was tall and skinny . . . the robe wrapped around her nearly double. She had straight black hair that fell nearly to her waist. She was olive-skinned, with pale blue eyes and an easy smile. She moved like a dancer.

"Do folks call you Harry?"

"Harrison," he croaked, realizing he hadn't used his voice in quite some time.

She frowned. "Harrison? That's a last name. Don't you have a first name? You've got Zachery—good old biblical name—Zach. Anybody call you Zach?"

"Harrison," he repeated with more strength, and wondered how the hell she knew his middle name.

She offered her hand. "Sara Peters."

He shook her hand and noticed the strength of it. This was a woman who knew work . . . hard work. This was a woman who might be capable of many things, like dragging an injured man to her cabin in the mountains, for instance.

"You must have a ton of questions," she said as she pulled the long hair back and in two moves pinned it up and out of her way. "Well, let's see . . ."

"Mama?" The call came from down the hall.

"I'm up, Liza," this Sara person called back.

So she had a kid . . . a girl . . . couldn't be all bad. "Get L.C. up and get dressed. School today."

Two kids.

"It's snowing," came a grumble from another room. "They be calling school off . . ."

"Not up here, Jefferson. Now get moving. And ask Ling to come in. Our Mr. Hixon has decided to join the world of the living after all."

She grinned down at Harrison as if they shared some wonderful secret and winked.

The next thing he knew he was surrounded. On the bed was a delightful little dark-eyed beauty of about five or six who studied him carefully. At the foot of the bed stood a tough little kid in Mickey Mouse p.j.s. At the door was a tall, scowling black teenager. And entering the room last was a young Asian man who was fumbling with his horn-rimmed glasses. God, what on earth had he stumbled on here?

"Good morning, Mr. Hixon. I am Dr. Ling Hu."

"Doctor?" *Right, fellow,* Harrison thought, *and I'm Prince Charles. The kid couldn't be more than twenty years old.* They shook hands. The intelligent thing seemed to be to play along with this madhouse—at least until he could find his clothes.

"You fell off your bike," the small girl, Liza pronounced importantly. "Mama says you were a damned fool to be there after dark. . . ."

He glanced at "Mama" who nodded her head in agreement. "That's right, Liza. And now why don't you and L. C. get your clothes on while I start breakfast?"

"Who's going to take care of him?" Liza seemed concerned but the mention of breakfast had her off the bed and headed for the door.

"Ling will take care of him. After all he's the doctor." Sara picked up some clothes for herself and shepherded the two younger children out of the room. "Come on, Jefferson, get your clothes on. I need you to run an errand."

That left Harrison alone with Dr. Hu.

Dressed in jeans and a flannel shirt, Sara started breakfast for the children. She needed to get out to the barn and see to the animals. She also needed to stay busy and stop thinking about the impact that a conscious Harrison Hixon had on her.

She hadn't thought twice about bringing him here. After all when she and Ling and the children had found him, lying unconscious on the side of the road, it hadn't even occurred to her *not* to bring him here. It had seemed perfectly normal to have Jefferson and Ling carry the man up to her room where they had all gotten their first good look at him.

"He's a mess," L. C. had announced on seeing the man for the first time in the full light.

Sara couldn't disagree. His clothes had been ripped and dirty. A large bruise was forming over one side of his forehead. His cheek was caked with dried blood from surface cuts and scratches, and he was cold and wet. At least his leg wasn't broken and they were able to remove the primitive splint.

Once she had sent the children to get ready for bed, she and Ling had struggled to get the unconscious man undressed and cleaned up. Sara had tried hard not to notice how really gorgeous Harrison Zachery Hixon, Jr. was as she helped Ling remove his clothes. He was tanned and covered with brown hair that had been lightened by the sun. He was slim but muscular—the kind of athlete's body she had always appreciated.

She had actually needed to order herself to concentrate on something else. *You're not some silly schoolgirl*, she had admonished herself as she turned her attention to his face while Ling worked off the man's soggy underwear and finished bathing him.

With his hair drying, she could see it was a rich mahogany brown with reddish highlights. The lack of gray had made her wonder about age lines around his eyes. Were they from laughter or too much sun or too much stress? She doubted the latter. There had been something about Hixon—even knocked out cold—that told her he lived a comfortable life. Something about him screamed Money! Breeding! Class!

He had a stubble of whiskers that gave him a decidedly rakish look, even when unconscious, and his mouth was set slightly crooked on what otherwise appeared to be a perfect face.

Together she and Ling had dressed Mr. Harrison Hixon of New York in a shapeless muumuu Sara had once bought on a vacation in Florida. It was the easiest thing to put on him. But he had looked ridiculous, and the children who had come back on the pretense of saying goodnight had collapsed in a fit of giggles at the sight of him.

As usual Jefferson had been the first to react. "What you got that man made up as?" he asked and then started to grin. L. C. and Liza began to giggle, and then Ling was also laughing.

Sara had frowned at the bunch of them. "Well, it's better than having him lie there buck naked," she said defensively. And with that she had sent them all to their rooms to get some sleep.

Now, as she cracked the eggs for breakfast, she smiled at the image. But she was having some second thoughts about her latest good Samaritan act. After all Harrison Hixon had not exactly been overwhelmingly grateful this morning when he finally woke up. A simple "thank you for saving me from dying of exposure," would have been sufficient, especially in light of the fact that last evening's rain had turned to snow. The man could have frozen to death.

"Jefferson," Sara shouted as she scrambled the eggs and rescued toast from the old toaster that no longer popped up.

"Right here." He poured himself some coffee and watched her.

"You should be drinking milk," she said over her shoulder.

"There's milk in the coffee." He waited a beat. "Sugar, too," he said with the hint of a grin.

Sara hoped that the smile was a breakthrough. Getting close to Jefferson had not been easy. He had only been with her for a couple of weeks, of course, but still . . . "Jefferson, we need to go back to where we were last night and pick up Mr. Hixon's bike and things, okay?"

"So?"

She dished up a plate of eggs, bacon, and toast and put it in front of him. "So, you eat while I take a plate up to our patient, and I'll send L. C. and Liza down. We'll go while they're having their breakfast. That way we'll be back in plenty of time for the school bus."

Jefferson groaned.

Sara ignored him and loaded a tray. She stood for a moment, puzzling. Coffee? or tea? Probably coffee—New Yorkers probably drank coffee, hot and strong and black. She poured coffee into a thermos and added it to the tray. "I'll be down in a minute," she said. A grunt was the only answer.

"Liza? L. C.? Breakfast . . . downstairs . . . now." As Sara headed upstairs, she heard the scampering which meant they had not even begun to get dressed yet.

"You'll need to stay off it for at least a few days. Then some limited movement . . ."

"You're not getting this, doc. I want a real hospital and—no offense—a real doctor . . . and I want both now."

Sara eased open the door with her bare toe. "So, how's our patient, Dr. Hu?" She put the emphasis deliberately on his medical degree and pretended she hadn't heard a thing. Still, the panic in Ling's expression was unmistakable.

"I'm afraid he is not happy with my work."

"Really?" Sara looked directly at Harrison and frowned. Then she dismissed Ling's concerns with a wave of her hand. "Well, some hot coffee and a hearty country breakfast should improve his disposition. Why don't you go on downstairs and get some food yourself. You had a long night, Dr. Hu. Mr. Hixon should only know how you saved him. Why, how you spotted him in that rainstorm, I'll never know. It was his good fortune, I would say." She refused to make eye contact with Harrison. Instead she took Ling by the arm and walked with him to the door. "Now, you go on and get some breakfast, and then I'll need you to stay with Mr. Hixon and the kids while Jefferson and I go and pick up his bike."

Ling nodded and gratefully exited the room.

"You left a two thousand dollar bike on the side of the road all night?" Harrison Hixon was clearly upset.

Sara wheeled around to face him, all trace of her chipper spirit and smiling chatter gone. "Sue me, okay? I had to make a choice . . . you or the bike. Right about now, it's obvious I should have thought it over more."

Harrison eyed her, decided not to respond, and then glanced toward the tray. "Don't get yourself in a sweat. What's that?"

"Well, down here in the backwoods, we call it breakfast."

"Can we cut the sarcasm, lady? I appreciate all you've done, but you have to understand something. I clearly need some real medical help." He nodded toward his leg, which she could see was badly bruised and swollen around the knee and ankle.

She walked over and pulled back the curtain. "Well, now you see, Harry, that rain that brought you tumbling down turned into a late spring snow while you were sleeping. Also we are close to two hours of hard driving on a good day from the nearest hospital that would even begin to meet your high standards. Dr. Hu has come out here to offer the people in these hollers their first real medical care in years. I would say you've been damned lucky he decided to do that.''

He computed her information as he wolfed down the meal. ''What's a holler?'' he asked around a mouthful of food.

''A *hol-low* would be the Yankee interpretation, I believe—a small valley in the side of the mountain; a level place in the hills.''

''Like here?''

''Like here.''

He poured a second cup of the steaming coffee and gulped it down. Sara watched in amazement—the coffee was scalding hot. This guy must have Teflon insides.

''What'd you say your name was?'' He set the coffee mug down and leaned back against the pillows.

''Sara.'' Maybe he would be all right after all. From what she had overheard Ling saying, it looked as if he was going to be here for a few days.

''Well, Sara, here's what we're going to do. First, you're going to get me out of this clown costume and into my own clothes—you did bring my pack off the bike?''

She just glared at him.

''You didn't stop to bring my things? Holy shit, are you out of your mind, lady? And don't tell me you had to make a choice—there's one knapsack—it's not exactly a steamer trunk.''

She tossed him the small pouch where they had found his wallet. ''We found this—we thought it was important to know who you were—in case you died and we had to notify the next of kin.''

He was rifling through his wallet, and she realized he was checking the contents. Now Sara was livid. She reached over and grabbed a twenty dollar bill that was sticking up. "Damn," she muttered. "I told Jefferson to take *all* the large ones." Then she calmly ripped the twenty into tiny shreds and sprinkled it like confetti over the astonished Harrison Hixon.

Satisfied that, for the moment at least, the man was speechless, Sara gave him her sweetest Southern smile. "Now, Harry, Jefferson and I are going to get your bike and other things. Then I'm going to take the kids down to the bus stop for school. I would suggest that you use the time and solitude for an attitude adjustment."

She picked up the tray and walked out. "Liza? L. C.? Now," she ordered. Actually by the silence she realized the children were probably already downstairs, but she needed an exit line.

She shut the door and was halfway down the stairs when something heavy hit the door of her bedroom. "It's Harrison, lady. Not Harry. And I want a doctor, or I'm going to take this place apart. You got that?"

Jefferson was standing at the foot of the stairs looking up toward the closed door and the raging voice.

"Are you ready to go?" Sara asked without so much as a backward look as she proceeded to the kitchen.

TWO

Ling and the two smaller children were eating breakfast in silence. Only their eyes communicated that they had heard the rantings of their patient.

Sara took her coat from the hook on the back door. "Jefferson, are you ready?"

The boy grabbed a piece of toast from the plate on the table and followed her out.

Whenever Sara needed to calm down, singing always helped. She started humming along to the radio almost before Jefferson had his door closed. "Come on, Jefferson, sing along," Sara urged as they drove slowly along the road, looking for Hixon's bike.

Fourteen year old Jefferson Powell folded both arms firmly across his chest and scooted closer to the door of the van. "I might have to be here, but I sure as hell don't have to sing no songs."

Sara Peters glanced in his direction and grinned. "Everybody's into making announcements this morning, I see. Well, that's one way of communicating. We all have our thing here and if that's yours, we'll learn to work with you. Now then, I'm to understand that singing is not your bag?"

"My bag? Next, you'll be telling me I got rhythm." Jefferson spoke through gritted teeth.

Sara gave him a look of interest. "I wouldn't know— have you got rhythm?" And then she burst into the old Ethel Merman song, bellowing out the words and providing her own accompaniment by slapping her hands in time against the steering wheel. Jefferson actually relaxed as he rolled his eyes toward the ceiling and shook his head.

"You crazy, woman," he muttered when Sara had paused.

"It's *you are* or *you're*, okay?" Sara corrected. When Jefferson shot her a look of disgust, she shrugged. "Hey, in this world if you want to get ahead you need to be able to speak the language."

"White people's language," he muttered.

"Unfortunately, yes," she said softly.

They drove in silence, and Sara turned her attention back to negotiating the narrow curving mountain road. With the snow covering everything, it was hard to locate the exact spot where they had found Hixon the night before. And when they finally did, it was no easy chore getting down to where the bike had landed and getting it back up without slipping down the hillside themselves. She found the knapsack as ordered—it was heavy and hardly the small parcel Hixon had indicated. It also had an expensive label and the look of being new, as did the bike in spite of its current bent condition.

On the way back up the mountain both Sara and Jefferson were silent, each lost in thought. Jefferson studied the road ahead. "Ling's a doctor," he said as if Sara hadn't known this.

"Resident," she said nodding and at Jefferson's quizzical look added, "Almost a doctor."

Jefferson nodded. "What's he doing with you?" he asked after a minute.

"Ling is going to live at the farm and spend the next several months working with the folks who live up in these hills like I do. It's a program the medical school offers. They believe it does the students good to actually get out and doctor, if you can imagine that."

"But how come he's gonna live with you? You all got something going?" Jefferson grinned at her knowingly.

"Yeah. As of about three days ago we have this friendship going. I like Ling, and he seems to like me. I have the space, and he needs a place to set up and stay." She shrugged.

There was another pause. "How come you take in all these people?"

"I like people . . . kids especially."

"Then how come you don't have kids of your own 'stead of taking in other people's?"

"That's a good question. Well, the fact is I'd like very much to have my own children, but I'm in my thirties and not married yet and . . . you know, time can run out for a woman."

"You don't have to be married to have a kid."

"No, some people don't. Me? I'm funny about things like that. I'd like to give any child of mine the whole package if I can—you know . . . mother, father, a home, family. Besides, it seems to me that there are enough children who need help already in this world. So, as long as I'm not having children of my own, I figured it might be neat to help out some who needed me now."

"How come you don't just get married?"

"Well, now I have this thing about hoping to someday meet somebody really special . . . somebody I can share all the things I like to do with. It just seems like it's not a real good idea to get married just to be married."

"Yeah, I guess." He gave her a long look. "You seem kind of happy . . . I mean for being alone with all these kids around."

"I am happy, Jefferson. I have a very good life. I used to dream about filling that old farmhouse up with a whole bunch of kids, and now I've done it. Maybe it's not the way I thought it would be in my dreams, but so what? Sometimes, as we get older, dreams change. That doesn't mean we can't make them come true."

She was getting far too philosophical for a talk with a teenaged boy. Still, it was the first really involved conversation she and Jefferson had had. It meant progress. It meant that after two weeks of grunts and silence, he was beginning to open up.

"So, you just go out and pick up stray kids or what?"

Sara laughed. "Well, it's a little more complicated than that. When my folks died, the farmhouse seemed pretty empty, so I started working with the county, taking in kids in need of a place. Over the years there've been quite a few in and out. Sometimes somebody hears of a kid who could use some help and they call me. Other times— like with you—I kind of take matters into my own hands."

When he didn't say anything for a few minutes, Sara added softly, "You know, Jefferson, this isn't forever . . . being with me. I know that and it's okay."

Jefferson pondered this information for a few minutes. "So, how'd you get Liza and L. C.?"

"Liza's parents died in a fire last year. She had four younger brothers and sisters who died, too."

"That's rough," Jefferson said.

"She needs some time. One day, Liza will find a real family." She paused for a beat to give him time to digest the information. "L. C. got left at a gas station about a year ago. He's been with me ever since. He started calling me 'Mama' almost from that first day, and I guess Liza just kind of picked it up."

"I noticed."

Sara glanced at him as she turned onto the gravel road that marked the last two miles of their journey—the road to the farm. "You'll get back with your mom, too, Jefferson," she said softly.

He had noted the turnoff and with it his bluster and swagger reappeared. "Just get this straight, lady. Like I told you when I came here, I don't do no chores, don't matter to me how many strays you drag in. You got that?''

Sara smiled.

They made it back just in time to pick up Liza and L. C. and drive back down to the end of the gravel road. The school bus came around the curve just as Sara got to the highway. She rolled down her window.

"Morning, Jim."

"How's it going, Sara?"

"How're the roads?" She knew from her drive to get the bike that they were wet but not slippery, but Jim would expect a little small talk.

"Not bad. We'll take it slow. This'll all be gone by this afternoon probably."

Sara nodded and waved as Jim pulled the bus door closed and headed for his next stop.

Back at the farm, Sara deliberately stayed away from the house for a while longer and went to tend the chores. It was something that needed doing, she told herself. Chores couldn't be put off—Harry Hixon or no.

She should have known the man would come with an attitude—being from New York, he had to come with an attitude. And arrogance. Any idiot who would think he could tackle the Smokies in March at night on a bike . . . well, it had to be sheer arrogance because the man acted like he had at least a little bit of good sense. And he was certainly old enough to know better—mid-thirties was her guess.

In rhythm to her work, her mind raced with a litany of the sins of her newest visitor. *Ungrateful* topped the list. That one she mentally chanted over and over like a mantra. There was also *imperious, presumptuous, overbearing,* and *rude.* It further infuriated her that his good looks had stuck in her mind.

"He's probably used to that," she grumbled. "Probably thought I'd fall over in a dead faint when he graced me with one of his smiles. Probably thinks Southern women are into fainting over a good-looking man.''

But he was a good-looking man who had kissed her like she hadn't been kissed in a very long time . . . like she'd never been kissed in her life. Sara attacked her chores with renewed energy, but nothing would push the memory of that kiss from her mind.

She had thought he was still out cold when she had moved to the bed to check on him. Ling had warned her about fever, and so she had used her hand to touch his cheek and forehead. He had been moving restlessly about, and she had considered holding him to calm him.

That's when her wrist had been suddenly captured in his viselike grip, and in an instant he had pulled her down and covered her mouth with his. She'd been able to break contact once and had felt her heart racing, her mouth open to grab some air, as if she were swimming in a race. And then his hand had tangled into her hair, forcing her down once again, his tongue probing and touching hers, his hands massaging her neck and shoulders. And between kisses he was calling for ''Catherine''.

For a moment she had actually given in to the sensation of arousal he evoked in her. It had been so long. But then she had come to her senses and placed both hands against his chest. That's when his arms had dropped suddenly like stones on the covers and his head had lolled to one side. That's when she thought he was dead. ''Lord, I've killed him,'' she had muttered aloud.

But then he had released a shuddering sigh of pure exhaustion, and Sara had echoed with a sigh of relief, the first full breath she had taken since the kiss had started.

Through the night she had bathed his face and arms and had laid a cool cloth across his forehead. When he seemed to rest easier, Sara had allowed herself to close her eyes. And then she opened them immediately, knowing she wouldn't be able to sleep.

She had given in to that kiss. If there was one thing

Sara Peters was, it was honest with herself. She had few illusions about her looks, her lifestyle, or her prospects for romance. And the truth was, in that moment, she had allowed fantasy to take over for the reality that had been her roots. In that moment she had been very glad Harrison Zachery Hixon, Jr., was out of his delirious mind and would never know what had happened.

Through the long night he had thrashed and tossed. Sometimes he mumbled. "Catherine" was the only word she caught. She alternately washed his fevered skin or watched anxiously as he slept, waiting for the next bout of restlessness or for any sign of change.

The rain turned to snow before dawn. She did not have to look out the window to know that; she could tell by the unique lightness that filled the room as if dawn were breaking. She pulled the curtain aside and watched as the snow came, glancing now and again at her patient who slept peacefully. Just before the real dawn, she slept.

This morning when she had awakened and had seen him open-eyed and studying his surroundings, her heart had gone out to him. He must be confused and frightened, she had thought. Of course, that had been before he opened his arrogant mouth, before he started giving orders, and before he started acting like the big city smart guy who had to talk slow and loud to the stupid hillbilly woman.

Now as she moved across the slushy path from the barn to the hen house, Sara glanced up at her own bedroom window. *Let him lie up there in that ridiculous muumuu til he rots,* she thought, gripping the egg she was collecting so hard that it splattered in her hand. "Damn," she muttered.

"Sara?"

She hadn't heard Ling and almost dropped the whole basket of eggs when he spoke.

"Dammit, Ling, you're going to have to stop sneaking up on me like that." Immediately she regretted snapping at him. "I'm sorry." She smiled. "Long night."

"You need some rest," Ling said.

"Why, Dr. Hu, are you doctoring me now?"

He smiled shyly at her teasing. "Speaking of patients, that leg of his is going to take some time."

"Define *time*." Sara stopped and waited. She wanted Harrison Hixon out of her life, and the sooner, the better.

Ling shrugged. "I would have to guess under the best of circumstances we would be talking a couple of weeks."

"Well, let's deal in reality. These are hardly the best of circumstances."

Ling nodded. "Three, maybe four weeks. His knee was badly twisted in the fall, not to mention the ankle. Both will take time."

"And we thought it was good he hadn't broken anything," Sara said ruefully. They both glanced up at the window. "Well, let's go see how the beast is doing after his time alone."

"Not well," Ling said, hanging back a bit. "I was just up there. He's calling for a phone, pen and paper, and coffee—hot and strong, I believe. He sent me to find you."

"Really?"

"He asked where your husband was. He thinks Liza and L. C. are your real children. I don't think he's decided yet what to make of Jefferson . . . or me." Ling grinned.

Sara laughed out loud. "That's the ticket, Ling. We'll just keep him off balance, and then he'll have to cooperate. The more he cooperates, the sooner we can move him out of here."

"Do you think there's a chance of getting him back to the university . . . to the hospital?"

A moment before it would have been her most fervent wish—to be rid of this *disturbance* in her otherwise unruffled life. But that wasn't Sara's style. She could not resist any human of any age who in her opinion needed help. And in Harry Hixon's case, help was needed. It was not his knee or ankle, but that surly disposition of his really bothered her. No, Mr. Hixon needed a lesson in perception . . . understanding . . . appreciation. Also it might do the children some good, having him around. Sara was a firm believer that the problems of the world could be solved if people would just learn to accept the differences they had with each other and move forward.

"Sara? Perhaps we should call someone." Ling glanced toward the window of the room where Harry Hixon waited. "Perhaps," Ling added, "you might wish to call a full-fledged doctor?"

"Ling, you're the closest thing to a real doctor the folks in these hills have seen in a long long time, but if it'll make you feel any better I'll call Doc Goodman. He's the vet."

"I'd appreciate that," Ling said, and for the first time Sara realized that in his calm, imperturbable way the young man was scared.

"Okay," she said and headed in the back door. Now she was concerned. Had she overestimated Ling's abilities? What if they shouldn't have moved Hixon? What if they'd done more harm than good? She didn't think they had, but maybe. . . . She reached for the phone.

"Doc? Sara. Well, I've got a little something here. . . ." And she gave him the bare details of the case.

"What was the durn fool doing on a mountain on a bicycle at night?" Doc bellowed.

Sara ran through the steps they had taken.

"The durn fool'll be fine, Sara. Just keep him in bed and quiet, and I'd say, he'll be all right. Keep a watch on his temperature. Got that Chinese fellow there now, don't you?"

"Yes, he's going to stay with me and get some experience with rural medicine."

"Still got the hoodlum?"

The whole mountain knew how Sara had brought Jefferson home after he had tried to snatch her purse in a Charlotte shopping mall. She had told the judge she would take responsibility if the judge would see that Jefferson's mother got the help she needed for a drug problem.

"Jefferson's going to be here awhile, Doc," she said patiently. "Listen, I'd better get back upstairs. Stop by later, if you're out this way, okay?"

"You be careful, Sara—always taking in down-and-outers. You're gonna get yourself in trouble one of these days."

"Okay, Doc." Sara smiled as she hung up the phone. No matter how old Sara got, Doc's concern never changed. "Ought to be married with kids of your own," he'd mutter whenever he stopped by and found her nurturing someone new. "Been long enough, Sara," he would tell her every time he left. Tomorrow he would get a chance to remind her again.

"Well, Ling, Doc seems to think we're doing all the right things, but if it would make you feel any better, why don't you call your advisor at the hospital and run the case by him? I think I'll take our patient some nice herbal tea."

THREE

Harrison Hixon sat on the edge of the bed and surveyed the room. Since he had clearly been deserted, he figured he might as well devise a plan of escape. He had heard someone in the kitchen a short time before, and then the back door had closed. Now the house was very quiet. No coffee, no phone, no pen and paper had been delivered.

He was pretty sure the woman had gone off somewhere with her kids. He still hadn't figured out how the black kid fit in or where the woman's husband was—probably off in the woods shooting some defenseless deer or rabbit for dinner. In the backwoods like this there were sure to be guns; he expected if he made it downstairs there would be heads of animals mounted on the walls, although there weren't any in his room.

It was a small room. The bed, which took up a lot of space, was an open canopy kind of thing made from some kind of tree branches—very rustic and yet with a certain artistic charm he couldn't ignore. The dresser was old—good solid wood construction. Carpentry was a hobby of his, and he appreciated the workmanship that had gone into the making of ordinary furniture pieces in times past.

On the dresser was an assortment of bottles and jars of

creams, a hairbrush, and an old fabric-covered box that seemed to be stuffed to overfull with trinkets—he saw a seashell and some old lace peeking out. The hairpins he had seen the woman use to whip her hair into that completely unattractive bun spilled out of what looked like an old baby-food jar. There was no make-up, lipstick, powder, or perfume, but it didn't surprise him from what he'd seen so far. Not that she was bad looking.

No, she wasn't bad looking at all. With a little make-up, a different hairdo . . .

He turned to check out the rest of the room. There was a wicker rocker with a chintz cushion. She'd been sleeping there when he woke; she'd stayed all night with him, he realized for the first time. He remembered the cool cloths and saw the basin on the nightstand. The nightstand also held the old-fashioned alarm clock, the lamp, and a photograph.

He rolled across the bed and picked up the frame. The picture was of her and a man. So here at last was the husband. He was young and good-looking in a pretty-boy kind of way. He held a guitar in one hand, and, of course, there was a big cowboy hat on his head. She seemed older than he did. Across the picture was written, "Sara, couldn't have done it without you. Love, Tommy Lee."

Tommy Lee. It figured.

He put the photo down and adjusted the stupid gown she had wrapped him in while he was unconscious. That brought up some interesting points—had she undressed him? And if she had, where was Tommy Lee during all this?

Across from him was the tiny closet. The door was partially open. Through the crack he could see shirts and jeans—could be anybody's. On the floor were sturdy hiking and work shoes. There was nothing to suggest a woman—no dresses or frilly blouses or soft sweaters. On a hook was a man's wool shirt.

Using the post of the bed to hold his weight Harrison tried standing. He tested his leg and immediately took pressure off it. There was damage—probably permanent given the quality of help he'd received. He held onto the bedpost and hopped toward the closet. By stretching he was able to snag the shirt. He tossed it onto the bed. Then he hopped toward the dresser—he hoped ol' Tommy Lee wouldn't mind his borrowing a pair of underwear.

He pulled open a drawer—hers, obviously. Here there were lace and frill. The only other place he'd seen such delicate lingerie was in a shop on Lexington Avenue where Catherine liked to stop. He held up a silk camisole— turquoise. With her coloring and that long black hair, the woman would be a knockout in this—lucky Tommy Lee.

"I don't think it's your size."

He was so startled at her sudden presence in the doorway that for a moment he let go his grip on the bedpost. He teetered for balance, putting weight on his injured leg and biting back the shot of pain that came with that. Then he found his grip again and wheeled himself around so he could at least land on the bed as he fell.

She stood by the doorway, a mug of something steaming in her hand, and watched.

"Comfy?"

"I could have killed myself," he said trying in vain to rescue some dignity from the situation.

She came into the room then and set the mug down on the nightstand. "You New Yorkers are sure dramatic, aren't you? You might have reinjured an already injured body part, but I doubt that it would have been fatal. Want some herbal tea?"

She sat down in the rocker as if prepared for a nice chat and nodded toward the mug.

Harrison pulled the stupid gown around to cover himself, noticing the way her eyes had settled on his exposed thigh.

"I would like—not necessarily in the following order—

my clothes, a telephone, some coffee, preferably laced with brandy, and your assurance that I can leave here without further bodily harm.''

"Okay. Clothes I can do. The phone is tricky. We've only got the one. It's at the foot of the stairs and I don't think the cord's going to stretch, but when Jefferson gets back from school we'll see if he can rig something up. He's very handy with electronics. Meanwhile, we could do a sort of relay thing with me calling and you telling me what to say and all. Coffee with brandy? Nope. Not at all what the doctor has in mind for you. You need rest and . . .''

"Lady, what I need is a hot shower, my clothes, and a phone. Now get Dr. Hu and Tommy Lee up here to help . . . what's so damned funny?'' When he had mentioned Tommy Lee, he had jerked his head toward the photograph and Sara had started to smile.

"I can get you Dr. Hu, but Tommy is in Nashville . . . I think . . . unless he's already left on tour.''

"Perfect. Your husband plays in a band—Grand Ol' Opry, I suppose.'' This was getting weirder by the minute. Harrison was beginning to think he'd stumbled into the middle of a very bad B movie.

Now she was laughing. He glared at her until she made an attempt to compose herself.

"Tommy Lee has played the Opry—but he's also played Vegas and even, I do believe, New York.''

She watched with a distinct pleasure as his dark eyebrows shot up in surprise and then settled into a scowl of disbelief.

"Perhaps you've heard of him . . . Tommy Lee Tucker?''

He shot another look at the picture. Tommy Lee Tucker was one of the hottest names in pop/country music. In fact, Harrison was very fond of his current hit, "Ebony Eyes.'' He turned his gaze on the woman before him. Her eyes were blue—pale blue. Her hair was ebony, but her eyes were incredibly blue and large and laughing at him.

"About that shower," he said gruffly.

"Oh yes, I did change the subject, didn't I?" She picked up the mug of tea and offered it to him once more. "Why don't you humor me and sip on this tea while I go and find Ling. I'm sure between the two of us we can help you." He took the tea, and she gave him one of those that's-a-good-boy smiles and walked toward the door. She had a nice backside, and in the jeans her legs seemed about ten feet long.

"From where I sit, any man who'd leave you alone in these hills is a damned fool. Tommy Lee should stay home," he said softly and enjoyed the way her back stiffened and her step faltered for just a second. He'd hit a nerve, a crack in that otherwise wisecracking controlled exterior. When she glanced back at him, she was frowning. He lifted the mug of tea in salute and grinned at her. He could have sworn she blushed, but she was gone before he could be sure.

Ling was in the barn, discussing animal husbandry with Amos Goodman.

"Doc," Sara said and they both turned. "Goodman," she added and offered her hand to the vet.

"Brought you something," Amos said after accepting her handshake. They all walked out to his truck, and he pulled a pair of crutches from the back. "They're adjustable." This was directed at Ling who nodded.

"Well, good ole Harry is going to be thrilled to see these. He seems to have this idea he's been kidnapped," Sara explained in response to Doc's puzzled look. "Why don't you take them up—both of you? I'll be up in a minute."

She followed them into the kitchen and started to pull out the makings for sandwiches. "Stay for lunch, Doc?"

Amos turned and winked. "I was hoping I had timed my visit just right, Sara."

Amos Goodman never visited unless it involved a meal, a party, or some irresistible piece of gossip. He and his wife, Lucy, were Sara's neighbors, living about a mile from her place. Sara had often babysat for their children—all seven of them. Now some of them would come by and stay with whatever collection of little ones Sara might have at her place.

For the last couple of years, Amos and Lucy had tried to play matchmaker for Sara, but she had withstood all their efforts. She suspected Amos had been prodded by Lucy to check out this new man, not that Amos had needed any prodding.

She made up a platter of cheese sandwiches and put some barley soup on to heat. She could hear Amos, Ling, and Harry moving around upstairs as she worked. She assumed the crutches were a hit. A minute later she heard the shower running. At least he would be in a better frame of mind after a hot shower. Also it probably would help that he would be able to put on his own clothes.

Stirring the soup, she listened to the sound of the water rushing through the pipes. The massage of the water would hopefully make him more relaxed. She was thinking that, before the kids got home, they ought to have a talk, especially if Doc agreed that Hixon should stay put for the time being.

The pipes rattled as the water was shut off. She thought about him drying himself, thought about the way his hair might look wet, thought about how the water would bead on his shoulders and back . . . "Ouch!" She had burned the side of her hand as she pulled the spoon through the soup and too close to the edge of the pot.

"Damn," she whispered as she dropped the spoon and turned to run cool water over the burn. It wasn't serious but it hurt. Well, it served her right, mooning over some man who'd not given her a civil word all morning.

"Lunch ready?"

Amos and Ling came into the kitchen and pulled out their chairs. They seemed to have taken an instant liking to each other, judging by the way they were laughing and talking.

"You don't really think he . . ." Amos said, almost choking with laughter.

"I'm sure. Mr. Hixon did not suspect." And Ling was fairly giggling.

"Okay, guys, what's the story?"

Ling deferred to Amos.

"Well, I'd agree with Ling here and his supervisor down there at the university—the man needs to stay put." Again the conspiratorial grin.

"Thank you, doctors, for that medical update. Now what's the real scoop?"

Ling could hold it in no longer. "He thinks Dr. Goodman is a medical doctor."

Amos had trouble talking through his own laughter. "You shoulda seen the way his eyes lit up when Ling and me came into the room—especially when I offered him the crutches."

"His relief was almost indescribable—here, at least was a true doctor." Ling trailed off in another fit of giggles.

Sara was smiling now, even chuckling as she imagined the scene. She knew Amos. He would have played it to the hilt. "And, of course, Amos, you set him straight."

"Can't help it if the man's too dumb to ask any questions. I checked his knee, checked his ankle, complimented my colleague here on excellent work in distressing circumstances. . . ."

Now they were all three laughing. That's when the pounding started. They looked up toward the ceiling.

"Guess he's not so dumb as I thought. Seems to have found another use for those crutches," Amos mused.

"Sit down and eat some lunch, you two." Sara put a

couple of sandwiches, some chips, and two mugs of soup on the tray. "I'll check on our patient."

The pounding repeated. Sara scowled at the ceiling and then picked up the tray. "Eat," she ordered the two doctors as she headed for the stairs.

Harrison was feeling better. In the first place this Dr. Goodman might be nothing more than a country GP, but he was the most normal person Harrison had encountered since waking up this morning. And he had brought the crutches, which represented freedom . . . of a sort.

Already the two doctors had helped Harrison get up on the crutches and make his way down the hall to the bathroom. What a relief! When he had indicated that morning that he had to use the toilet, the woman had provided him with an antique chamber pot. She probably thought that was a nice touch. He'd actually been concerned that the only facilities might be an outhouse. He'd been lying there picturing the half-moon on the creaky old door for the last half hour.

But now things were looking up. Hu and Goodman had helped him into and out of the shower, had found his clothes, and had helped him get out of the clown get-up and into a pair of shorts and a t-shirt. He felt like a new man.

Now he was ravenous—he hadn't eaten enough of the breakfast she had brought. He had felt so lousy. And finding himself in this lunatic bin a hundred miles from God knew where hadn't helped his appetite.

He could hear them down in the kitchen which he surmised was just below his room. Technically, he guessed it was her room, but now that he was back in bed—clean and in his own clothes—he was feeling territorial. He could smell the soup or stew or something she was cooking. His stomach growled and still she did not come. She was down there laughing and talking with the doctors. He could imagine the scene. There would be the big old country table, homemade bread, stew or homemade soup. . . .

He picked up one of the crutches and banged on the floor. All talking and laughing ceased for a long second. Then he heard the low murmur of voices and dishes clinking. He heard the scrape of chairs and the sounds of people sitting down to eat. He banged again and heard the two men laugh, heard her voice calling something back to them as she came up the stairs.

"You banged?" She asked when she reached the room.

"Cute," he said, eyeing the tray.

"I'll get you a bell—so much more genteel, you know." She set a plate on the bedside table and watched as he swung himself to a sitting position and attacked the food.

"Hungry?"

For an answer he glanced at her and started on his second sandwich.

"How did it go with the crutches?" She settled into the rocker and bit into a sandwich she'd brought for herself.

"Great. Thank the doc for me again, will you?" Feeling magnanimous now that he considered himself more in control, he added, "And tell Dr. Hu I'm sorry for giving him such a hard time."

"He understands. After all, he's just graduated at the top of his class from one of the finest medical schools in the country, done his internship at a highly rated hospital complex, entered his residency in rural medicine in a program that's largely experimental . . . all that in spite of offers to practice in some of the leading research and teaching hospitals in the country. I mean, you stack that up against Doc's thirty years' experience . . ."

"All right. I said I gave the kid a hard time. But he'll learn a lot working with Dr. Goodman—experience counts."

Sara nodded solemnly. "It does at that. But I'm not sure delivering a baby is the same as delivering a calf—

although there are similarities to be sure. And when a horse does to his leg what you've done to yours, well, more often than not the only choice is to shoot him. Still . . ." She wrapped her fingers around the mug of soup and allowed the steam to waft over her face. She closed her eyes and waited.

A beat later, the light dawned. "Are you saying . . . good grief, the man's a veterinarian? What kind of God-forsaken, backwater, primitive . . ."

"Some people might use those very words to describe your own New York, Mr. Hixon."

"I want a phone and I want it now. Have you got that, lady?"

She stood up then and picked up one of his crutches. She raised it over him and he actually flinched. "You see this? Get the other one and get off your backside if you want a phone so desperately. I told you it didn't reach up here. The stairs are this way. Oh, and be very careful. Since you're insisting on managing them before you're ready, please don't say I didn't warn you. I really can't afford a lawsuit."

And with that she strode out of the room. He heard the sound of her shoes on the stairs and then, "Ling. Amos. I'm going for a walk." Then the back door slammed and all was quiet again. He decided the phone could wait. She was probably right.

The next day, Harrison saw little of Sara. His meals were delivered by Jefferson with a silent sullenness that did not invite inquiry. And his other needs were met by Dr. Hu.

Not that Sara wasn't around. He would hear her, as well as the two younger children, off and on throughout the day. She passed his . . . actually her . . . room at night on her way to put the children to bed but did not stop or look in.

Harrison spent much of his time sleeping. The accident had really taken a lot out of him. Beyond the injuries to his knee and ankle there were assorted bruises and aches and pains to heal.

The next day promised more of the same. Sara stayed away. Ling and Jefferson were dispatched to deliver food and assist him to and from the bathroom. He spent a lot of time sleeping and by late afternoon was wide awake and restless.

He could hear sounds from the kitchen: preparations for another meal, children talking, the occasional sound of an adult voice. Sara's. He could tell that she had been back in the room—things were always different after she'd been there. The crutches stood at the ready, next to the bed. Once she had unpacked his knapsack, storing the clothes and leaving the paperback novel on the bedside table. This time she had left some sports magazines, apparently noting that he had finished the novel. There, too, was the telephone. Finally! His eyes followed the cord that ran across the room and out the door.

Someone came into the kitchen from outside—Jefferson, judging from the voice. What was a woman who had two small children and a traveling husband doing living in the back woods and hosting the likes of a teenager and a foreign exchange student?

For that matter, what was she doing living in a place like this? He knew at least a little about the entertainment business, and if he was any judge at all, Tommy Lee was bringing in a bundle of money.

He reached for the crutches and maneuvered himself into a standing position. Not bad. He'd been smart to get himself in top condition before attempting this trip. The years of working to stay in shape had paid off. He should heal pretty quickly. The knee was stiff but that was to be expected . . . he hoped.

He carefully made his way to the bathroom, passing what he surmised to be a room for each child along the way. With each trip he took in a little more of his surroundings. The voices came from the kitchen, which seemed to be back under the stairs and under the open balcony that overlooked the great room below. He had to admit that the place had its charm—rustic to be sure, but definitely pleasing. The furnishings were a mix of antiques and traditional, accented by artwork and handicrafts that added to the country feel of the room.

He heard the woman talking from the kitchen and paused to listen.

"After supper, Jefferson, would you help me get the sofabed set up?"

"Ling going to sleep there?" There was an element of hope in the boy's voice that made Harrison smile.

"No, it's for Mr. Hixon." Then softer she added, "I really appreciate your sharing your room with Ling for a couple of nights, Jefferson. Amos is sending somebody by tomorrow to help fix the pipes in the cottage. As soon as we can get some running water out there, Ling will have that for his office and living quarters."

Harrison wondered if she had put her arm around the boy as she told him this. The comfort in her voice implied it. With Jefferson, her voice was as soft and appealing as it had been strong and sarcastic with him.

He reluctantly moved away from the family drama and went on into the bathroom.

FOUR

When he got back to the room, she was sitting in the rocker. She had set up his food tray on a snack table next to the bed. For herself she nursed a mug of coffee.

"Thanks for the phone," he said as he eased his weight onto the bed, trying hard not to lean on his injured leg, trying hard not to let her see him grimace as a shot of pain raced through his body.

"I thought we should talk," she said with no acknowledgement of his comment. "What do you do, Mr. Hixon?"

So she was still upset with him.

"I'm an attorney."

"Defense or prosecution?"

"Neither. Corporate." He started to eat. It was a delicious dinner—rice and broccoli and chicken in some sort of stir-fry. "This is good," he said nodding toward the plate.

"Thank you."

They sat in silence for several minutes, and she watched him eat. He tried not to mind.

"You got any more questions?" he said finally.

"One or two."

"Such as?"

"Well, the one that seems to come up with everyone who hears about you is what on earth were you doing on a mountain in March after dark on a bicycle?" She said it calmly, ticking each point off on her fingers as if she needed to be sure to get it all in.

He smiled, even gave a sheepish laugh. "Pretty stupid, huh?" Usually he hated anything that made him look less than in full charge.

"I don't know. If your intent was to get yourself killed or commit suicide, it wasn't the least bit stupid—it was more of a sure thing."

"I'm not usually so naive. I had some trouble with the bike earlier in the day—kept having to stop and make repairs, adjustments. It cost me in time. I lost a couple of hours in some little town at the foot of the mountain. . . ."

"Tate's Mill," she supplied.

"I needed a particular part. Anyway, I guess I have a problem in that I set schedules—deadlines—it comes with my work. Maybe it's hard to leave it at the office. I had set a schedule to be a certain distance each day, and I had lost a lot of time. . . ."

"Do you know anything about mountains, Mr. Hixon?"

"It's late March. I'm in the South. I figured it'd be springtime."

"It is springtime. But in the mountains—any mountains—spring can mean a glorious sixty-five degree day followed by a sudden storm, rain turning to snow, slippery roads. And speaking of roads, we don't spend a lot of money on lighting them down here."

He gave her a wry look. "I noticed."

"The point is you were lucky we came along."

"Where were you coming from?"

"The children and I had been in Charlotte to do a show and then on our way we stopped by the university to pick up Ling—Dr. Hu."

"You sing, too?" He glanced toward the nightstand and saw that the picture of Tommy Lee had been moved.

"I am an artist and sometimes antique dealer. I travel to several shows each season. When they can, the children help. This was an opening at a gallery in Charlotte."

That explained the antiques in the living room.

"What kind of art?"

"I'm a weaver—fabric, wallhangings . . ."

"I'd like to see some of your work." He saw the way she looked up sharply, her eyes bright with skepticism. "Really," he added.

"Perhaps tomorrow you can come downstairs. I've asked Jefferson and Dr. Hu to help me set up a place for you there." She did not look at him as she picked up the tray and headed for the door.

"I'd like that. And I'm sure you'll be glad to get back in your own bed."

"You can make any calls you like, Mr. Hixon. Just please reverse the charges." She gave him a look to make sure he got the message. "I'll send Dr. Hu up to have a look at your leg," she added.

He didn't want to let her go yet. "Tell me about the bed," he said before she could leave.

She glanced at it as if it were nothing unusual. "It's willow," she offered and then shrugged.

"Who made it?"

"A friend—another artist. We traded. I did some wallhangings for his studio, and he did this for me."

"It's unusual. I like it."

She stared at him, searching for hidden meanings and then said simply, "Thank you," and once more turned to go.

"Sara?"

He knew it was the first time he had called her by name. She knew it, too. Actually that had been his purpose. He hadn't the vaguest idea what he meant to add to that—

just wanted to test the sound of her name. Luckily, he didn't have to come up with anything.

"Mama, I finished everything on my plate." The little girl stood just outside the door. She was talking to Sara, but her eyes were on Harrison.

"Hi," he called, and it was clearly the only opening she needed.

In the next minute she was on the bed. "I'm Liza. You're Harry. Will you read me my bedtime story tonight?"

"Liza, this is Mr. Hixon to you, and I've explained to you that he is not feeling too well."

Liza focused on his leg. "You got an owie."

He grinned at her. "A major owie," he said. Then he looked at Sara. "I'd really enjoy doing the story thing, if you wouldn't mind."

And that's when the calm cool demeanor of Sara Peters collapsed. "The story *thing*? Lord help us. You're not only from the city, you're a Republican."

"That's a fairly major conclusion to jump to from one simple choice of phrasing," he said with a frown. "Besides my politics are . . ."

"None of my business?"

They were back to square one—sparks flying between the flinted looks. Liza measured the situation, looking from one to the other. When L. C. came into the room, she said solemnly, "Mr. Hixon is a 'publican."

L. C. glanced at the man in the bed and back at Sara. "What's a 'publican?" he demanded.

Sara registered his presence for the first time. "It's Republican, and it's someone who believes . . . different things than I do."

"Like in church?"

"Well, not exactly," Sara faltered.

"It has to do with voting . . . elections," Harrison said. "Have you studied that in school?"

"Sure. I got nominated to be class president, but Roger Meadows beat me. The girls really go for Roger."

"Sometimes that's the way it all works out," Sara said with a defiant look at Harrison. "People get fooled into choosing based on surface things like looks and TV commericals."

"You, I take it, are a Democrat," Harrison said.

"I'm your worst nightmare, bucko. I'm not only a Democrat, I'm a *liberal* Democrat. See how easily the L word trips off my tongue? Come on, kids, time to get your baths and into your p.j.s. Mr. Hixon needs to make some calls."

When they had gone, Harrison picked up the phone. Who to call? No one was really expecting to hear from him for several weeks. Greg, his partner, had suggested the time off. Greg's wife, Nancy, had seconded the motion. "You need a break, some time to regroup, Harrison. It's been long enough, and if you're going to get on with your life, I think you need to get away and just think it all through."

His parents were just back from Europe, and he saw no need to alarm them. At his own co-op, there was no one to answer his call—only the machine. He mentally ran through other friends he might contact and rejected each as either not close enough to bother or too much of an alarmist to handle the information. He finally called his doctor's office and left word with the service for Tom Watson to call him back.

He laid back on the pillows and focused on his leg. He tried a couple of tentative flexing exercises and stopped when pain was his reward. He sighed and glanced around the room again. She had said they would move him downstairs—that would help. These walls were starting to close in. He felt someone watching him and looked toward the door.

"Hi, Harry." Liza accepted his look as an invitation to come in. She climbed up on the bed and presented him with one of three books she struggled to carry. She was freshly bathed and dressed in a floor length pink nightgown, her hair in damp ringlets around her cherubic face. "This one," she said and settled back on the pillows next to him.

"Ah, Dr. Seuss—my personal favorite." He opened the cover and began to read. As he got into it, he developed a range of voices to delight and charm Liza. He was rewarded with her giggles and punches from her tiny fist to his side.

Her laughter eventually attracted L. C. who at first sat on the rocker, pretending nonchalance in his Batman p.j.s and slicked back hair. But soon he came onto the bed on the other side, and the three of them moved through the other two books, taking turns making up the voices and accents of the characters.

Sara stood outside the room for some time, listening. It was past time for the children to be in bed, but she couldn't bring herself to interrupt. The laughter that rolled out of that room was magic, especially because she knew there had been little enough of it in either Liza's or L. C.'s life.

In spite of herself, she had smiled a couple of times when one of Harry's accents was particularly bizarre. She found herself picturing the way his face would contort to achieve a specific sound and then how it might break into a helpless smile as the children collapsed in giggles. He didn't even seem to mind them calling him Harry. Of course, who could resist Liza's coquettish, "Oh, Harry."

"They gonna keep that racket up all night?"

She hadn't heard Jefferson come out of his room.

"I got homework, you know," he added testily.

"They're going to bed now," Sara answered. "You having trouble?"

"Math." Jefferson said the word as if it alone encompassed an answer.

"Oh." Sara couldn't really offer much help. Math had

been her own worst subject in school, and at this point she'd forgotten everything she learned anyway. "Maybe Ling can help," she suggested.

"He's gone over to Doc's to borrow some tools for working on the cottage tomorrow."

She knew that and had forgotten. "When he gets back maybe," she offered and moved toward the door and the sounds of laughter.

"Maybe he can help," Jefferson suggested, jerking his head toward the room where Harrison was.

"I wouldn't bother him. . . . Well, maybe it wouldn't hurt to ask."

Jefferson grinned and turned back to his own room for his books.

"Time for bed, you two—past time."

She was met by choruses of protest. "Now don't start. You're wound tighter than a drum, but there's school tomorrow and chores . . . just like always. Now, scram. Oh, and what do you say?" She nodded toward Harrison.

"Thanks, Mr. Hixon," L. C. said solemnly as he slid off the bed and headed for Sara. She bent to give him a hug and kiss.

Liza planted a loud kiss on Harrison's cheek and hugged him hard. "Thanks a bunch, Harry. You're the best story reader I ever met." Then she fairly danced out of the room.

"I'll be right there," Sara called. "Get in bed . . . both of you."

Giggles and running feet were the only answer.

She glanced at Harry. "Thanks."

"No problem. I enjoyed it—made the time pass for one thing."

"Did you make your calls?"

"I'm waiting for a call back," he said.

She was curious but couldn't ask. "Well, if it rings, go ahead and pick up—it's the only other phone in the house.

There's one in the barn, but . . .'' She was rambling and wondered what was the matter with her.

Jefferson stood at the door and cleared his throat. Harrison looked his way and frowned.

"Oh, yeah," Sara jumped in. "If you're not too tired, Jefferson was having some problems with his math homework. I'd help but it's pretty advanced for me, and Ling's gone over to Doc's for some—"

"Let me take a look," Harrison said, and Jefferson moved into the room. He handed Harrison the book, pointed out the page, and took a seat in the rocker.

Sara felt dismissed. "I'll go check on the kids," she said, but neither of them seemed to hear or notice when she left.

After Jefferson left the room Harrison lay back and thought about his predicament. Having had some sports-related injuries in the past, he tended to agree that the best idea was to stay put and give his body time to heal. Still, he was in a position that left him with few choices and little control. He wasn't used to that. Up to now his life had run on his schedule. For the last two years he hadn't had to answer to anyone else before deciding how to spend his time, and he'd grown somewhat accustomed to that. Even recognizing that he had given up quite a bit by not becoming more intimately involved in the lives of others, he wasn't unhappy—lonely sometimes, but not unhappy.

Sara Peters, on the other hand, seemed to operate her entire life on the basis of other people. She was surrounded by them, and from all appearances she was deeply enmeshed in their lives. She was not unlike his mother.

Elizabeth Hixon was always involved in several projects at once. She had been that way ever since Harrison could remember. From the time he was small, at least a part of the time with his mother had been spent protesting or revamping some issue she deemed important or in need of their help. It had been very flattering and more than a little overwhelming to have her seek his opinion about the "right thing" to do in whatever project she was involved with.

It was probably the source of his own political and personal conservatism, he mused. A childhood interspersed with protest marches in place of Little League and dinner conversations filled with arguments about strategy instead of "How was your day, dear?" could be very intimidating. Not that he didn't admire his mother—his father as well. For two of the very upper crust society of New York, they had never taken their wealth and position for granted. And the one thing they had taught all their children was social responsibility.

"I do not agree with your viewpoints most of the time," his mother had said to him, "but I respect the fact that you do believe them. There is a place for anyone who thinks an issue through and tries to resolve it with honor and dignity."

"Why, Mother, are you saying that it's possible for a conservative to be right?"

She had laughed at that. "Oh darling, you're no conservative—a moderate perhaps—but coming from this house you could never be conservative in the truest sense of that word."

He couldn't argue with that.

"You know when I married your father, he thought he was a conservative, too. We used to have the most engrossing discussions. And look at him now." Elizabeth had beamed with pride at her husband. Clearly he was her finest cause.

Harrison frowned.

Sara Peters had made political assumptions about him that held no water. If she only knew. She would certainly be surprised if she could meet Elizabeth. Of course, the two of them would probably be totally in tune with each other. He suspected Sara shared some of his mother's inflammatory and unorthodox viewpoints about what was wrong with America and how to fix it.

He noticed how his thoughts kept coming back to Sara, which, of course, was perfectly logical given his current situation in her house with her as his only contact with civilization.

She had a way about her that was both charming and infuriating—one minute all softly feminine and maternal and the next a mountain lion prepared to do battle to protect any perceived threat to her domain.

He heard her pass the door on her way downstairs. She did not stop to say goodnight, though she must have seen the light. He wondered why that should disappoint him, decided he was simply bored, and turned off the light.

They were all asleep when the phone rang. Sara was downstairs on the couch. By the time Ling had returned, Harrison was asleep and she had decided to postpone moving him until the morning. The phone, however, was still next to Harrison's bed. "Of all the inconsiderate . . ." she muttered, expecting this was the return of Harrison's earlier call. She fumbled for her watch and saw that it was just past one.

She heard the low tones of his sleep-coated voice as he answered and hoped he would let the person know that one did not make phone calls at this hour, especially to a farm. She buried her head beneath the pillow and willed herself back to sleep.

"Sara?"

She thought she was dreaming at first.

"Sara?" The whisper became a hiss . . . louder, insistent.

She uncovered her face and looked up. Harrison was standing on his crutches at the balcony. "It's Tommy Lee. He's asking for you."

She got up and headed for the stairs. Harrison waited until she got to the top. "He sounds drunk," he added with clear disapproval.

She moved to the bed and sat on the edge as she picked up the phone. "Tommy?"

"Who the hell was that?"

He was drunk or high or both. Drugged to be sure. "Ah, Tommy," she almost whispered it, her disappointment was so great.

At the sound of her frustration, Harrison eased himself back into the room in case she needed him. He balanced on his crutches and the highboy dresser just inside the door. Her back was to him. Her hair, loose now and tangled from sleep, covered her face, but her body language spoke of dejection, failure, defeat.

"Hi, baby." A giggle. She recalled the innocence of Liza and L. C.'s laughter earlier and cringed.

"Where are you, Tommy?"

"I'm on the coast, baby. . . ."

"Stop calling me that. Who's with you?"

Tommy Lee became suddenly contrite. "Aw, don't be mad at me, Sara. I know I've been bad again, but—"

"Is anybody with you, Tommy?"

"Sure, there's a goddamn party . . . can't you hear?" He apparently held the phone out to pick up sounds—loud music, lots of loud conversation. . . .

"Tommy, listen to me." Her voice was soft but firm. It commanded compliance.

"I'm listening." It was a whimper. Then softly, pleadingly, "Help me, Sara."

"Is Warren there?" Warren was Tommy's manager—a no nonsense accountant type who kept the many facets of the rocketing career of Tommy Lee in check.

Another giggle. "Warren? Here?"

"I didn't think so. I'm going to call him, okay? He'll come get you, okay?"

No answer.

"Tommy?"

Harrison heard the panic in her voice. There seemed to

be a long beat during which she held her breath and then let it out slowly.

"Did you hear what I said?"

"Warren . . ." Tommy sounded sleepy.

"Stay there, okay? Warren's coming."

"Warren's coming," Tommy repeated like a robot.

Sara pushed the disconnect button and dialed the operator. "Get me the Beverly Hills Hotel," she said.

Harrison marveled at the facets of her—one minute all business, the next the consoling earth mother, and then again with him, the sharp-tongued overseer.

In minutes she had located Warren—whoever he was— and filled him in. Clearly Warren was reliable. She hung up and continued to sit by the phone. Harrison waited.

"Is there anything I can do?" he asked after a minute had passed and she hadn't moved.

"Yeah, sit down over here, before you fall down. I just have to wait for Warren to call back."

Harrison moved to the rocker. In sleep his leg had stiffened, and he was more than happy to sit down.

"And Warren is?"

"Tommy's manager."

"Tommy is drunk?"

She pushed her hair back with one hand and looked directly at him for the first time since picking up the phone. "Tommy is bombed out of his skull." Her eyes flashed in the light from the nightstand. The woman was furious.

"I'm sorry," he muttered and wasn't sure why.

Defeat replaced the anger. "No, I'm sorry. It's not your fault." She stared at the phone, willing it to ring.

"It'll take some time," he said softly understanding that she was waiting for Warren to get to wherever Tommy was and assess the situation.

"I'll make some tea," she said, standing up, agitated, needing to make the time pass.

He reached out and took her hand. "Why don't you

wait here? It won't take that long. Tell me about Tommy.'' He noticed again the tight, well-muscled body, silhouetted now in the light from the nightstand. She was wearing a gown not unlike the one Liza had on earlier, but on her it was provocative instead of charming. He thought about what it would be like to touch her, and his thumb moved involuntarily along her palm.

For a moment she stood there mesmerized by the erotic massage of his thumb against her palm. Their eyes met, and he thought about kissing her. Then she pulled away and turned to the closet, pulling the chenille robe from a hook and wrapping herself in it. She busied herself with straightening items on the highboy, her back to him.

''Tell me about Tommy,'' he repeated.

Her hand paused in mid-action. Then she turned and looked at him directly.

''We aren't married, you know.''

FIVE

It was worse than he thought, and his face must have registered his disapproval. Not that he was a prude, but given Tommy Lee's financial windfall and the way Sara seemed to be living from one art fair to the next, it did seem to be a less than equitable relationship.

"You're . . . living together." He searched for words that would not offend.

"Well, not at the moment, but yes, for a while Tommy was here."

Harrison could not have explained the sudden anger he felt toward the man. "I'm sorry," he said after a moment.

Sara, unable to keep up the act one minute longer, burst out laughing, her hand partially covering her mouth, her hair falling over her face.

Oh, great, Harrison thought, *now I've made her cry*. He made a half move toward her and was brought up short by the pain in his ankle and leg when he put weight on it.

"Look, Harry, don't reinjure yourself. Trust me, this isn't worth it."

She was dry-eyed and smiling as she moved closer to the bed, one hand outstretched as if to break his fall.

When he sat down on the edge of the bed, she sat next to him.

"It's this way—Tommy is one of my kids."

"He's your son?" Impossible. He was a pretty good judge of age and in the most extreme scenario the woman was no more than thirty-five. Tommy Lee was in his twenties—that would mean she'd been pregnant at . . . no. On the other hand, this was the South, the hill country. . . .

"Harrison, pay attention. I don't have any children of my own—Tommy, Liza, L. C., Jefferson, and the others who've come and gone are like foster kids. I sort of take them in for awhile until they can get back on their feet, and then I send them on their way. In Tommy's case, it may have been too soon." She glanced toward the dresser where the photograph now sat and added pensively, "On the other hand, with Tommy a lifetime may have been too soon." She shook her head.

"He was drunk tonight?"

"Drunk . . . doped up . . . with Tommy it's usually a combination. That's how I got him here. Sixteen years old and stealing big time to support a habit. But that boy could sing—he has such talent, such gifts." She shook her head in wonder. "Did you know he writes most of the stuff he does? Not just the words but the music?"

"Are you going out there—to L.A.?"

She focused on him once again and once again laughed. "Honey, I can't afford a cab fare to downtown Tate's Mill, much less a plane ticket across the whole country. No, Warren will handle it. He's good with Tommy. He'll get him the help he needs. I'll talk to Tommy in a few days. He'll call again."

"You've been through this before."

"Success has been hard for Tommy. At first he just gloried in it—all that love coming across the footlights. All those fans meeting every plane, every bus. But now he's beginning to understand that it's not real . . . that kind of love. It's just for the moment. He already had that kind of love from his parents—you'd think he might understand.''

"Tell me about Liza and L. C.''

She turned so she could lean against the post at the foot of the bed and brought one knee up to rest her chin on. "That Liza is a beauty, isn't she?''

"She certainly seems fearless.'' He smiled as he recalled the evening's bedtime story session.

Sara turned suddenly serious. "She actually has many fears—many terrors. One night while you're here, I'm sure you're going to wake to her screams. She has nightmares—not as much as at first, but still now and then. There was a fire. Her parents and siblings all died. She plays a pretend game that she has convinced herself is true that one day the family will be together again—that everybody else is just away for awhile.''

"How'd she get out?''

"She had gone downstairs to get her doll. She didn't know the fire had already started—a smoldering cigarette in the couch. When she tried to go back upstairs, the hall and stairway were filled with smoke. She tried to cry out and couldn't. Somehow she got outside and ran to a neighbor's, but by the time help came, the others were all dead.''

"Jesus, didn't these people ever hear of smoke alarms?''

"They had one in the house, but her parents had removed the batteries to use in a toy for one of the kids.''

"How long has she been with you?''

"About a year now. Several months ago a couple from Charlotte thought they wanted to adopt her but then decided her fears and nightmares were more than they wanted to tackle.'' There was a bitterness in this last statement and Sara'a face set in a hard protective way.

He was quiet for a moment, waiting for her to go on. When she didn't, he prompted, "And L. C.?''

She looked at him, perhaps to gauge the level of real

interest. "Well, one day Liza was in the van with me, and we had stopped for gas. At the gas station, there was the sheriff's car and a couple of people from social services I'd gotten to know pretty well. L. C. had been left there. He kept telling everyone it was a mistake—that they would be back. Then Liza took a long look at him and said, 'They aren't coming back. Come on home with me and Sara.' The sheriff and social services agreed and that was sort of that."

"And they call you Mama?"

She smiled. "L. C. started with that almost immediately. I tried to insist on Sara—even Auntie Sara—but he stood his ground. Liza just picked it up from him. You'll notice Jefferson doesn't call me that."

Harrison frowned at the mention of Jefferson—he was trouble. In spite of his obviously quick mind, maybe because of it, Harrison viewed the boy as a potential danger. "Amos mentioned that you got Jefferson through some deal in a courtroom—a purse snatching?"

She stared at him through narrowed eyes. "So, you were pumping Doc?"

He shrugged. "I had to know what I was getting into here."

"You didn't have a whole lot of choice—you still don't, judging by the fact that your own people haven't even bothered to call back."

"You're changing the subject." She made him uncomfortable, staring at him like that, examining each expression that crossed his face. He felt spotlighted in the lamplight while she sat at the foot of the bed, half in shadow.

"Maybe you're the danger," she said, her voice quiet and serious. "Maybe I was foolish to bring you into our home. Maybe when you're better you'll murder us all in our sleep and steal away with the family silver. Do I have to worry or not, Harry?"

He gave a frustrated sigh. "Why do you insist on

Harry? Is it too much to ask that you call me by my given name?''

''Harrison? It's pretentious. Are you trying to tell me you went all the way through school with no nickname?''

''Harrison is a perfectly legitimate name.''

She shrugged. ''Well, it doesn't fit. Maybe back in New York, in your big office and three-piece suits, it fits, but not down here. Nope, that's my price for taking you in— Harry or out you go. What's your pleasure?''

She didn't seem very interested in his answer since she chose that moment to stand up and arch her back in a stretch. ''God, I'm bushed. I wish Warren would call back so I could catch at least an hour's sleep before dawn.''

His respect for her grew. This woman was on her own, and the farm was no hobby, nor was the weaving. ''You handle this farm by yourself?''

''It was my parents' place. Since they died, I've leased out most of the fields and pastures. When I'm on the road, I have some arrangements with neighbors to look after the animals and such.'' She shrugged as if the whole lifestyle were perfectly normal.

''And you can make a living on rent from leased fields and selling your wares at art fairs?''

She bristled. ''Well, I'm sure it wouldn't come up to the standards you may be accustomed to, but it suits me.'' She began to pace.

He felt annoyance at her assumption that he came from money just because he came from New York. Of course, the fact that he did come from money made her assumption all that much more irksome.

''I just meant . . .''

As if on cue the phone rang. She answered it before the first ring had ended. ''Warren? . . . Yeah. . . . Okay. . . . Sounds like the right choice. . . . Good night, and give Tommy my love. . . . Yeah. Thanks.''

''Is this your life?'' Harrison asked again as she hung

up the phone and replaced it on the bedside table. "I mean, what about . . . kids of your own, a husband . . ."

She glanced at him, and he was sure she was preparing some angry retort. But she just grinned and patted him on the head like one of her brood of stray kids. "Now, Harry, that's enough for one night. You've been talking to Amos entirely too much. You get some sleep. I'll see you in the morning."

The following morning she orchestrated his descent downstairs immediately after breakfast. Jefferson and Dr. Hu formed a sort of chair by grasping each other's arms and carried Harrison down to the sunroom just off the kitchen into which she had moved a reclining chair. "I'll bring the rest of your things down later." Then she turned to Dr. Hu. "Ling, I'm going to drive the kids to the school bus and go on to pick up some supplies. Do you need anything?"

"No. Doc is coming by to bring some supplies for finishing the cottage and to introduce me around. I think I'll be out most all day unless, of course, I can be of help here." He glanced at Harrison.

"Hey, guys," Harrison spoke up just to remind them he could still think and speak. "I'm okay. Got everything I need right here." He indicated the crutches.

Ling and Sara looked at him skeptically. "There's a bathroom through there. Food's in the refrigerator. I'll be back as soon as I can," Sara said then moved back to the kitchen. "Kids? Move it."

There was general pandemonium as the children gathered in the kitchen and looked for coats and homework and lost books, and Doc arrived to drop off the supplies and pick up Hu. There was a rumble of engines and a scattering of gravel as both vehicles left. Then suddenly the house was quiet. Harrison was alone.

He took the crutches and began his survey of his sur-

roundings. The kitchen was chaos—the leavings of breakfast and other projects scattered everywhere. Harrison was
a man of order, and he could not resist closing cabinets
and drawers as he made his way toward the living room.

Actually it was more of a great room and seemed much
cozier than it had from the balcony. One wall was almost
totally glass soaring two stories to give a spectacular view
of the mountains. The snow was gone and there were
actually patches of blooming things to be seen. This was
the North Carolina spring he had imagined.

On either side of the fieldstone fireplace were book-
shelves overstocked with books—classics and contemporary, craft books, books about marketing and business, an
encyclopedia set, a home medical guide. Books were piled
on top of each other, and shelves curved at the center
under the weight.

Sara's loom stood in the corner facing the mountain
view. He examined the work that hung on the walls and
draped the sofas. He was taken by the contemporary styl-
ing with that hint of something far more lasting. Perhaps
it was her use of color that hinted at mountains and forests
and water. Or maybe it was the use of line and texture.
He was no authority, but he was certain her work would
bring major money in New York.

Outside the windows, a large deck ran the length of the
house. He saw the handmade rockers that matched the bed
upstairs in her room—willow she had told him. They were
sturdy and charming. There was also a swing in the same
style. He imagined her there on a spring night—perhaps
wrapped in one of the shawls she had made—sipping coffee. He saw himself there with her and knew that the
sounds of the mountain, which had been so unnerving
when he was on his bike alone, would be enchanting from
Sara's front porch.

He moved past the dining table and china cabinet, noted
a small television on a rolling cart stored under the stair-

way, and headed back for his room. Her hand was everywhere he turned—in the flowers that bloomed in profusion in pots on every window, in the soup that simmered slowly on the back burner of the ancient stove, in the hooks for coats inside the back door, each mounted at a height that matched each child.

The sunroom looked out toward the outbuildings—a small barn, perhaps a chicken coop given the profusion of chicks in the area, and the place where Ling would have his office and apartment. And then he saw his bike.

The front wheel was missing, and the frame was covered with mud. It was too distant to tell whether there had been damage. One toe clip dangled precariously, and the handlebars were set at a peculiar angle. He thought of the investment he had made and realized his focus had been too much on weightlessness and not nearly enough on sturdiness. He realized that despite all the reading and research he had done, he had selected his most important companion on this trip as a novice.

The phone rang. Harrison hobbled to the foot of the stairs to answer it.

"Harrison? Greg." As if his partner and best friend had to identify himself.

"How's it going?" Actually, he wondered how Greg had gotten this number.

'How's it going?' Are you for real? "Watson called . . . said you left a message. He had to leave for Hawaii—medical conference—and thought I should check on you. Are you all right? Nancy's about to have a heart attack she's so worried."

"I had a little accident—nothing life threatening." He gave Greg the bare details, playing down the crutches, putting the emphasis on damage to the bike. "So, I'm here until I can make some repairs."

"And where's *here*?"

"The town's called Tate's Mill."

"Quaint." Greg was a city person, born and bred. The

charms of the rural completely mystified him. "Are you in a hospital there or hotel or what?"

"I'm staying on a farm with some people I met. One of them is a doctor. The woman who owns the farm is a weaver and antique dealer."

"A doctor and his wife—well, that sounds a little better." Greg sounded enormously relieved and Harrison recognized the thought process. A doctor and his wife meant education, time spent away from the attitudes he imagined were cultivated like a cash crop throughout the region. Yeah, Harrison had had those same thoughts.

"Well, no. They're not married. The doctor is a Chinese man who's doing a specialty in rural medicine. He just has a room here."

"And the woman?"

"She's a weaver and antique dealer."

"You said that. Not married?"

Harrison could hear Nancy in the background and realized Greg was calling from home. Any time there was the remote possibility Harrison might be moving back into the world of male/female relationships Nancy was interested.

"She has a bunch of kids," Harrison added as if he hadn't heard the question.

"Oh." Greg was disappointed. "I get it."

Harrison grinned. He knew Greg very well. His friend would take the sketchy information he had provided and come up with a mental picture of a middle-aged farm woman, fat and weathered with a bunch of brats hanging on her skirts.

"So, what's the plan?" Greg asked.

"Well, I'll stay here until I can get the bike fixed. You don't need me back there, do you?"

There was a pause.

"Actually, the Reynolds matter has been moved up."

The Reynolds case was their biggest ever. It had been that case that Harrison would return to at the end of the month for final preparations.

"How far up?"

"Just a week. I hate to ask but maybe you could cut the trip short by a week?"

Harrison heard the muffled protests of Nancy in the background, and then Greg was back on the line.

"Or we could work on it by phone. What do you think? How long will you be there?"

Harrison looked at his bruised knee and badly sprained ankle. "I could get a plane . . ."

"No. That's not necessary. Come on. We all agreed you needed this. Look, you're not going to be any good for us if you haven't finished working things through, right?"

Harrison smiled ruefully. "You'd just like me to work a little faster and be back a week early."

He heard Greg chuckle. "Well, yeah. On the other hand, if you could stay put there for a few days . . . a week tops . . . we could do a lot."

"Sounds like the best plan," Harrison agreed.

"Okay." Greg sounded relieved. "I'll call you from the office. You wouldn't happen to be near a fax machine, would you?"

"I don't know. Unless there's one out by the outhouse," Harrison said thoughtfully.

Again, there was a pause. Then Greg laughed nervously. "That's a joke, right? I mean, you are joking? There is indoor plumbing?"

"Don't get hysterical. There's indoor plumbing. I'll check in town and see about a fax, okay?"

"Okay. I'll call from the office. Wait, Nancy wants a word."

Before Harrison could protest, Greg had handed the phone to his wife. "So, how are you, really?"

"Fine . . . really."

"Tell me about the woman."

"Now, Nancy, she's a very nice woman. Her name is Sara Peters . . . I'm not sure of her pedigree." Nancy came from old money and Social Register status. Harrison teased her constantly about it.

"And she's a widow?"

"No."

"But she has children?"

"Yes."

There was an exasperated sigh, then Nancy said, "You aren't going to tell me a bloody thing, are you?"

"When I get home, I'll tell you all about my adventures in the hill country, all right?"

"Those adventures had better include at least one night of mad passionate lovemaking. Do you understand me, Harrison?"

"Goodbye, Nancy."

He spent the rest of the morning on the phone. He found the phone book in a kitchen drawer and used the Yellow Pages to call around until he located a fax at the local newspaper office. Greg called from the office, and Harrison gave him the fax number so he could send a copy of the file. They made arrangements to talk the following day.

While he was on the phone Sara returned and busied herself upstairs. Then she came through with a huge pile of linens and started doing the laundry. While the washer ran, she was outside tending to chores in the barn. Every time she passed as he was on the phone, he could see that her curiosity was aroused, but she never interrupted or asked for any explanation.

So, at lunch he gave her one. He told her all about the call from Greg, about Greg and Nancy, about the Reynolds case.

"I could pick up the fax tomorrow," she said. "What time?"

"I asked Ed Bower to call when it came into his office there." He had met Ed via phone that morning. Ed was the editor of the local paper. Again, Harrison had been struck by the man's evident intelligence and sophistication. He commented on it to Sara as they ate their salads.

"Well, imagine that," she said in her best imitation of the simpering Southern belle. "A real ed-u-cated man right here in Tate's Mill? I don't believe a word of it. You all are just funning me, now, aren't you, Mr. Hixon?"

"All right, you made your point. I just meant to say that perhaps there's been some misconception about people who live in this part of the country."

She assumed her normal voice. "No. Really? Prejudice up north? In the city? Where they know everything?"

He had never considered himself a prejudiced person. "Listen, lady, I've done my share of demonstrating for rights and civil liberties, so don't . . ."

"Oh, please," she said as she cleared the dishes. "The next thing you know you'll be telling me some of your best friends are black." She went upstairs, and he could hear her putting clothes away.

"Well, they are," he shouted.

The phone rang. He'd carried it into the kitchen so he could spread out his work on the table. Still exasperated with Sara, he practically ripped the receiver off its base, "Hello."

It was his doctor from New York, calling from the airport in California as he waited for his connection to Hawaii.

By the time he had gone through the litany of his injuries and the treatment he had received to date, plus exacted a promise from Tom Watson not to reveal the extent of his injuries to anyone, the house was quiet. Quiet, except for a rhythmic sound of board against board and the beat of what seemed to be screens being raised and lowered.

"Sara?" No answer.

He picked up his crutches and moved through the kitchen toward the sound.

She was sitting at the loom, her back to him. She was wearing earphones, and she seemed to keep time to whatever music she heard. She was weaving, her feet working the pedals that raised the screen-like panels, her hands sending a shuttle back and forth and between each pass pulling hard against the board that pushed the threads tightly together.

He stood in the doorway and watched her, knowing she was unaware of his presence.

She started to sing along with the music he could not hear. She had a deep rich voice, and her head and shoulders moved in concert with the music. Her hair was pulled back and braided in a no-nonsense way. Again, she was dressed in the jeans and sweater that seemed to be her uniform. She had removed her shoes and worked the loom with bare feet. There was something incredibly sensual about the slimness of her ankle as she played the pedals of the loom. He had an urge to move closer, to stand behind her, to release her hair and let it fall over her back as it had last night.

Instead he turned back to the kitchen. He washed and dried the dishes she had left to soak and stacked them on the counter. He wiped the table and straightened the chairs. He looked around for more to do and seeing nothing he could manage, went outside.

Sara wove every afternoon. She allowed herself one afternoon a week off except when there was a show or something that was really important—like going to pick up Ling the other day—but otherwise she stuck to her routine. She was not a disciplined person by nature, and she knew that only by establishing a regular time and routine would she finish what she needed for the coming season of art fairs.

She'd already had her day off this week—Harrison Hixon had seen to that. She'd devoted entirely too much time to him. He wasn't hurt all that badly after all. It had only been that first night. Probably a slight concussion, Amos had said. But the lasting damage was a badly bruised knee and sprained ankle.

Normally Sara was happy to take in anyone who was in need of help, but normally people were grateful . . . appreciative. Even Jefferson, for all his toughness, occasionally reacted with pleasure.

Harrison acted as if all this were somehow her fault, as if she had planned to stumble across him lying on the side of the road, as if there were some hillbilly plot to kidnap him and keep him here against his will.

Like he was such hot stuff.

She pumped the treadles to raise the harnesses and create the shed, and with a practiced hand she expertly sent the shuttle flying through the tunnel of warp yarns. Then simultaneously she released the treadles and slammed the beater against the row of weft she had just created. She repeated each step in rhythm, building the pattern with each shot of the shuttle, each beat against the weft. Her hands and feet worked without conscious direction leaving her thoughts free to ramble.

So, Harrison Hixon was bright, she thought.

Treadle . . . shuttle . . . beat . . .

So, he wasn't bad looking.

Treadle . . . shuttle . . . beat . . . beat again . . .

So, he had this way of focusing on a person when they were talking like that person was the most incredibly interesting human he'd ever met.

Treadle . . . shuttle . . . beat . . . again . . . and again . . .

So, his eyes were deep set and penetrating and dark with multiple messages, even secrets.

Sara pulled the beater hard and looked at her work.

It would have to all come out. She'd been beating so hard that the area she had been working on stood out from all the rest like the mistake it was. This piece was supposed to be light and delicate, like the clouds that floated over the mountains outside her window.

With a sigh, she removed the headphones and began the tedious job of undoing what she had woven. Once again Harrison had intruded.

SIX

By the time she redid the work on the loom, it was almost time for the children to come home from school. Through the afternoon the house had been quiet, and she had assumed Harrison was sleeping. But when she looked in on him on her way through the kitchen, she found his room empty. Hearing noises from the cottage Ling would use as an office and apartment, she headed outside.

It was a glorious spring day—great billowing clouds in a sky of Carolina blue. Overnight it seemed as if the daffodils and first tulips had opened. Suddenly it was spring—really spring. A person couldn't help feeling good on a day like this, no matter how many Harrison Hixons were around.

"Ling?"

She stepped onto the small porch of the cottage and looked inside. In the second it took for her eyes to adjust to the sudden shade, she realized the figure bent over the tool box was too large and too muscular to be Ling.

"So, here you are," she said brightly. She had decided while redoing her weaving that the only sane way to deal with Harrison Hixon was to treat him exactly as she would any other visitor who stopped by the farm for a day or so.

"Why didn't you tell me the bike was totaled?" It was an accusation, and Harrison did not look up as he continued to rummage through the toolbox.

"Are you looking for something in particular or just banging around in frustration?" She took a seat on a stool near the door.

The truth was Harrison didn't know a damned thing about bike repair beyond the rudimentary changing of a tire or replacing a chain. It wasn't her fault, after all, that he had set out on this adventure so ill-prepared.

He sighed and eased himself down on the floor near the bike. "Banging around in frustration," he said and then smiled. "Sorry, I didn't mean to take it out on you."

He had actually uttered an apology—perhaps there was some hope for him yet.

"I can imagine this is all pretty disappointing. I mean, you start out on a nice vacation, make plans, have time commitments, people to see. . . ."

"Well, I can't say it hasn't been an adventure," he said and smiled again. "How's your work going?" At her quizzical look he added, "The weaving."

She shrugged. "Not one of my better days. Too much spring in the air, maybe."

"You have a nice place here—very peaceful."

"Thanks."

They were quiet for a moment. He looked around at the work Ling had started. "I could give Ling a hand with this," he said.

"I'm sure he'd appreciate that."

He looked at her and grinned. "You're skeptical?"

"Well, I guess it would surprise me to find you knowing your way around a toolbox, yes."

"I may not know much about repairing a bike, but I can wield a hammer and screwdriver, not to mention a paintbrush."

"I'm impressed."

"Truth is I'm used to being busy, so if it's okay, as long as I'm here, I'll make myself useful." He pulled himself up by supporting his weight on a table.

Sara caught herself studying him and liking what she saw. He was the most virile and intelligent man she had met in a very long time. Over the years the really bright and interesting men in the area had either gotten married, moved away, or both. Generally Sara's social circle these days consisted of people considerably younger or older than she was. She was finding it a bit disconcerting dealing with someone who was her equal. She found herself responding to Harrison in ways she had not acknowledged for several years.

"Sara?"

He'd been saying something, and she'd gotten so lost in her own thoughts she hadn't heard him. Now he was standing near her, balancing on the crutches, his face very close.

"I'm sorry, what did you say?"

His eyes held hers. "Actually, I asked you where I could find a paintbrush, but what I meant to say is how very glad I am that it was you who found me the other night." His voice was low, seductive, enticing.

Sara swung toward the door and hopped off the stool. "Yeah," she said as she went out onto the porch, "it could've been Amos who found you. I'll get you that brush." She knew her voice was too bright, too loud, and she noticed how the spring air seemed to fill her lungs as if she had been without it for too long.

He ate supper with them that night—one big family around the kitchen table, Sara noted ruefully. After all, didn't most households sport three displaced or orphaned children, a Chinese med student, a New York lawyer and . . . her. Who was she in all this?

"Harry?" Liza's voice penetrated the general conversation.

"Mr. Hixon," Sara corrected automatically.

Liza rolled her eyes toward the ceiling and continued. "Are we reading tonight?"

"I don't see why not. L. C., are you going to join us?"

L. C. glanced toward Jefferson to register his reaction to this conversation. He did not want to appear uncool in the eyes of the teenager.

"Just keep it down," Jefferson muttered.

L. C. took that for permission and beamed back his answer to Harrison.

"Then it's settled." Harrison raised his glass to Sara in a mock toast. "Will you join us, Mom?"

Suddenly everyone became very quiet and all eyes swerved to Sara. *"Mom* wouldn't miss it, Harry," she replied and raised her own glass in more of a challenge to him than a toast.

He grinned and went back to eating.

"You know, kids," he said after a moment. "I was thinking. Dr. Hu here really needs that place of his ready for action—not to mention that Jefferson would like his room back . . ." He glanced at the teenager who was looking at him in surprise.

"Maybe we could all work together and get that place all set by Monday—use the weekend as a sort of work party, what do you think?"

There was a hum of response around the table, some positive, some grumbling.

"I would very much appreciate the help," Ling offered.

"I'm in," Jefferson grunted and turned his attention back to the food, but not before Sara noted a slight smile.

"Me, too," L. C. said, taking his cue as usual from Jefferson.

"Then we're decided. Maybe the womenfolk could rustle up a picnic to break up the work. What do you say?" Harrison focused on Liza, knowing full well he was on the receiving end of daggers from Sara's eyes.

"A picnic? By the creek?" Liza adored the creek, and

since she wasn't allowed to play there unaccompanied, she found any reason to go there cause for celebration.

"The creek sounds nice," Harrison said. Then he risked a look at Sara. "Okay?"

"Why, Mr. Hixon, us womenfolk would be just charmed to spend a beautiful spring day all shut up in the kitchen putting together a picnic for you big strong he-men." It was her Scarlett voice again.

The children giggled. Ling looked confused. Harrison grinned and then matched Sara's accent. "Well, that's just great, ma'am. Sure do appreciate your hospitality. So, Ling, just what all needs doing—let's make a list."

The rest of the meal was taken up with animated conversation about the conversion of the cottage. Everyone had their own ideas about how best to get the job done—everyone except Sara. She just sat back sipping her coffee and considering the way Harrison Hixon was slowly but surely taking over her house.

Later after the stories were read and the children were in bed and Ling had retired to the living room to catch up on some reading, Harrison found Sara sitting alone on the porch.

"You missed the story hour," he said as he pushed open the screen door.

"I listened from out here," she said, her back to him as she sat on the step and considered the stars.

"Beautiful night," Harrison noted easing himself down next to her.

She didn't answer.

"You aren't mad, are you? I was just kidding around, you know."

Again, that voice, low and velvety, working its way into her thoughts, probably into her dreams.

She looked at him. "Would you like me to check on getting you a flight back to New York tomorrow?"

"Whoa, you are mad."

"No," she said softly. "I've just been thinking that maybe you thought you were stuck here. There is an airport in Charlotte, a really nice one with flights to most anywhere."

"I know I can get a plane, Sara." He waited a beat. "Do you want me to go?"

"That isn't the issue."

"And that isn't an answer," he noted.

"I just thought since your trip has been spoiled—I mean you obviously started out on some sort of . . . planned schedule . . . and now with this big case coming up . . ." She shrugged.

"Can I tell you about this trip? I mean maybe it will help you understand that I am not usually so . . . ill-prepared."

She shrugged again and waited. She was finding it increasingly difficult to look at him. Every time she did she noticed something she liked, something attractive, something inviting. Like now, he was sitting so close, their shoulders were almost but not quite touching. And the way he used his hands when he talked made a person notice what strong hands they were.

"My wife died two years ago," he said quietly.

Suddenly Sara's eyes were riveted on his face. Now he was the one studying the stars. His face was in shadow.

"I'm sorry. She must have been very . . . young."

"Yeah, well. Anyway, afterwards I pretty much buried myself in work—became a real Type A personality, not that I wasn't already. Catherine was, too."

Catherine. So, this was the Catherine he had called in his delirium that first night. This was the Catherine he had kissed when he kissed Sara.

"What kind of work did she do?"

"She was an actress—Broadway, national tours, that sort of thing."

"She must have been beautiful."

"Yeah."

There were beats between each exchange. He was lost in thought, and she considered how much to ask.

"We had been planning a trip," he said suddenly. "Right before it happened, we had made all these plans. We talked about seeing other parts of the country—how it would do us good to get out of New York."

"You grew up there?"

"Born and raised," he said smiling at the stars.

"But you must have traveled."

"Oh, sure. But mostly out of the country. My folks had . . . have . . . money. When we took a family vacation it was to an island or to Europe."

"Catherine?"

"She came from California."

"So, this is a sentimental journey—the one you meant to take with Catherine?"

He was quiet, then finally he shrugged. "That's one way of looking at it."

She had an urge to put her arm around him, to hold and comfort him as she had the children who had passed through her life. Instead she said again, "I'm sorry, Harry."

"Actually this particular trip was my partner's idea. Greg and his wife, Nancy, have been nagging me for months to get way. When I finally agreed, Nancy was beside herself." He turned to look at Sara for the first time since mentioning Catherine. "You know, she's absolutely dying to know about you."

"Me?"

"Yeah, Nancy's a born matchmaker—been trying to fix me up for the last year. When she heard about you, I could practically hear the wheels turning."

"What did you tell her?" Now it was Sara's turn to look away.

"At the moment, she's pretty sure you're a fat, middle-aged widow woman with a houseful of kids."

"Hardly the stuff of perfect matches for the likes of you." Sara had no idea why she was feeling so hurt.

"That was the idea," Harry said quietly, and she could feel him studying her face. Then he reached out and touched her hair. "If I'd told her the truth, she wouldn't rest until she had us . . . together."

She wouldn't look at him, but he saw how her eyes closed for a moment, how she sat perfectly still and did not move away from his fingers touching her hair.

"I'd like to stay for awhile, Sara."

She looked at him then and saw sadness. He was still thinking of Catherine. He was looking for Catherine on this trip. Sara had been down that road once before; she wasn't about to make the same mistake again. She stood up, which had the effect of his hand falling suddenly to his side.

"Of course. Stay as long as you like. You know, I believe Ling knows a little about bicycle repair. You might speak to him tomorrow. Goodnight, Harry."

He had been dismissed. Almost before he could get out a "goodnight" of his own she was in the house. He heard her say something to Ling and then go up the stairs.

But he hadn't imagined her response . . . no more than he had invented his own. There was an attraction here, improbable as it seemed. He had been that close to kissing her . . . and she had been that close to letting him. Harrison was certain of it. He frowned and went in to talk to Ling about the mangled bike.

On Saturday, the work party turned out to be more fun than Sara would have thought possible. The children followed Harrison's orders as if he were some sort of Pied Piper. By noon they had the cottage thoroughly cleaned and the first coat of paint on the walls. Harrison and Ling were painting the trim while Jefferson replaced a board in the small front porch. The two younger children had been given the job of washing out the paintbrushes and were hard at work getting as much paint as possible on themselves.

"Sandwiches," Sara called as she pulled open the screen door, balancing a tray in one hand.

"Food," Harrison called and all three children came running.

"I thought we were gonna do a picnic," L. C. said as he bit into a sandwich.

"This is a picnic," Harrison replied before Sara could answer.

"Not by the creek," Liza protested with a frown.

"Well, I had an idea," Sara said, and they all turned their attention to her. "I was thinking that since the work is going so well, why not have our picnic by the creek at suppertime and make it a celebration?"

The children were immediately enthusiastic.

"We could do games," Liza decided.

"With prizes, maybe," L. C. added with a look toward Sara.

"Maybe some fireworks." This last surprisingly came from Ling, who smiled shyly and simply shrugged his shoulders when they all looked at him in disbelief. "Perhaps," he said again and went back to his food.

"How about a parade?" Sara suggested.

"With costumes?" This was Liza whose favorite game was dress-up.

"Costumes? No way." Jefferson had been quietly going along with the flow of things until now.

"Oh, Jefferson," Sara cried in mock protest, "I have the perfect thing for you."

"No costume." Jefferson was adamant.

"Well, all right. But if you wouldn't mind I could use your help with L. C. and Liza, okay?"

Jefferson just looked at her for a long minute and then grunted.

"I'll take that as a yes," Sara said. "Now, Harry, can you and Ling finish this place?"

"We'll need a little help with moving the furniture in, but otherwise. I think we can manage, right, Ling?"

Ling nodded and grinned.

"That reminds me," Sara said, "Reverend Thompson called. He and Amy will be over later to help us move furniture. He has a desk he said he'd like you to have."

"Miss Thompson is coming? Here?" L. C. blushed several shades of pink and then raced out of the cottage.

"Wait," Liza called and took off after him.

"Miss Thompson is the minister's daughter . . . and L. C.'s teacher," Sara explained. "He has a major crush on her."

"She's a fox all right," Jefferson mumbled.

The adults glanced at him and then laughed.

"Well, she is," he protested and then scowled at the three of them. "Hadn't we oughta get started if we're gonna do this picnic?" And with that he deposited his soda can on the tray and strode out to the porch.

"Sounds like Amy Thompson has more than one admirer," Harrison noted.

"My kids have good taste," Sara said with a grin. "Will you guys be okay for awhile? I've got something I need to work on and then I can give you a hand."

"With all due respect, Sara," Ling said solemnly, "the most help you can offer is to occupy L. C. and Liza—we find ourselves having to redo their work." Then he smiled and winked.

"Gotcha, Doc."

Reverend Donald Thompson and his daughter, Amy, arrived in the late afternoon. By the time they had unloaded the desk and carried the other furnishings from the house to the cottage, it was clear that Amy Thompson had collected yet another heart. Ling Hu was absolutely smitten with her if Sara was any judge at all.

"That business about spring and a young man's fancy

seems to have international implications," Harrison noted when Sara came out to see how things were progressing.

"I noticed."

"Seems the feeling is mutual." Harrison nodded toward Amy who was looking at Ling as if he were sent directly from heaven.

"Uh, Sara, I have to meet Mrs. Thompson at the church. . . ." Don Thompson wiped his hands on a bandana hankerchief.

"Oh, I was just going to invite Edith here, so you all would join us. We're having a picnic supper by the creek."

"Sounds nice. But, we can't."

"Well, at least let Amy stay. We haven't had a chance to talk yet, and the children really like seeing her outside of school."

Thompson thought the idea over.

"I'm sure Ling could see her home," Harrison added.

"I'll ask her if she'd like to stay," Thompson said.

Judging by his daughter's beaming smile, the answer was yes. The minister gave Sara the high sign and headed for his car.

"Give my best to Edith," Sara called.

"See you in church," the minister answered and then chuckled.

"Okay, let's get this show on the road. Children!" Sara walked through the house gathering supplies for the picnic. "Parade time. Line up."

Bedroom doors opened all along the balcony, and the three youngsters appeared. L. C. was wearing his Batman pajama top and a black mask Sara had found in the attic. He had a pillow case pinned to his shirt like a cape. Liza was radiant in her nightgown, a piece of cheesecloth fashioned into a veil, and train and a pair of high heeled shoes from the back of Sara's closet.

And Jefferson was incredible. Sara had shown him how to make body paint from cornstarch and food coloring, and he had completely decorated his face with geometric designs in red, blue, and yellow. He was even smiling.

"Are we ready?" Sara asked.

"Yes," shouted the children as they clattered down the stairs and lined up by the kitchen door.

"You need a costume, if you're gonna be the leader," Jefferson said to Sara.

She glanced around until her eyes lighted on an old felt hat that had belonged to her father and that she sometimes wore when it rained. "How's this?"

"Good," squealed Liza.

"We need a drum," L. C. said.

Sara grabbed the empty soup pot and a metal spoon and presented them to L. C. Then she picked up the broom from the corner and twirled it like a baton. "First, to the cottage," she announced as she cradled a brown paper package under her free arm.

Harrison, Ling, and Amy were just clearing the last of the trash and the tools when they heard the clatter of the metal drum and the children's laughter.

"Dr. Ling Hu?" Sara intoned it like a town crier.

Ling and the others moved out onto the porch.

"Ah, Dr. Hu, I presume. Company, halt," shouted Sara above the din of the drum. "Thank you."

Harrison watched as she made a production of presenting Hu with a handpainted shingle to hang outside his office. She must have worked all afternoon on it. Heaven only knew when she had time to also put together a supper and costume the kids. All Harrison seemed capable of at the moment was standing there and grinning at her. He couldn't remember feeling so good about the events of one day in a very long time.

"To the creek," Liza cried in perfect imitation of Sara after Ling had made a short acceptance speech.

There was nothing to do but fall in line. Harrison

grabbed his crutches and hobbled along behind Amy and Ling.

After supper, the children received permission to play in the creek. Even Jefferson wandered down and, seeing fish, ran back to the barn for a pole he had seen there.

Amy and Ling walked off toward the woods, their heads bent close in conversation. Amy had been fascinated with Ling's work and especially the idea that one day he hoped to practice medicine in China. "I've always wanted to see China," she had said softly.

Harrison watched as Sara busied herself with clearing the picnic. "Come over here and sit with me for a while," he said when the silence between them had become too obvious.

She glanced at him, but continued to gather the empty containers.

"It's been a wonderful day, Sara. Thank you."

She didn't look at him, but he noticed the way her busy hands skipped a beat. "You're welcome." Finally, she ran out of things to do. When she looked up, Harrison smiled and patted the grass next to him.

"Now, will you light somewhere for five minutes?"

She smiled and sat down, leaning against the tree, keeping her distance from his lounging position just a foot away. "Thanks for all your help," she said. "It really means a lot to Ling to be all set up for Monday, ready to play doctor."

"He's a good man."

They sat listening to the squeals and chatter of the children. Sara relaxed. She loved this time of day—the sunset, the dusk.

"Sara?"

She had closed her eyes, savoring the breeze, the sounds of the coming night, the delighted cries of the children. "Mmm?"

"How come you've never married?"

Her eyes flew open. He had moved closer. He was

sitting quite near . . . too near. "How do you know I haven't?"

"I asked Amy Thompson."

Sara was practically sputtering. "You what? How . . . what . . ."

"Actually, she brought it up. She mentioned how somebody who's as good with kids as you are—how it's a shame you never married—I agreed. I mean, you are incredibly good with these kids."

She recognized a compliment of sorts and, since she had never known how to take a compliment, was momentarily quiet.

"It just seems to me that not only are you too good with kids not to have any of your own, but you're far too bright and attractive and talented to spend your life hidden away in these hills." Again that voice—quiet, soothing, captivating.

"It's my choice," she said softly but knew her voice was ineffectual.

He took her hand and traced a pattern in the palm of it with his finger. "I was thinking last night about why I wanted to stay for a while."

All she seemed capable of was watching his finger mark its design on her palm.

"I think, Sara, that I have to stay until I've at least kissed you once. What do you think?" He put her fingers against his lips. "I find I'm thinking about kissing you quite a lot lately." He kissed her wrist.

Sara closed her eyes and remembered when he had kissed her that first night, when he had dreamed of Catherine. She remembered his mouth on hers and how she hadn't been able to forget that kiss. Without opening her eyes, she knew his face was near enough now. All she had to do was give in. . . .

"Mama!"

It was a shriek of panic not play, and immediately Sara was on her feet and running toward the creek. "Ling," she shouted toward the woods and saw Ling and Amy come running to meet her.

They all arrived at the creek at the same time. Liza was crying hysterically, blood gushing from her foot. L. C. was crying also as he raced along the bank calling for help. "Liza," he shrieked. "Liza."

Jefferson had removed his shirt and was wrapping Liza's foot to stop the bleeding while he cradled the girl against his chest. His eyes, too, were wild with panic.

"Get my bag," Ling said quietly as soon as he had knelt next to Liza and Jefferson. Amy raced back toward the cottage. "It'll be all right," Ling said soothingly. "Let me just look."

He started to remove the blood-soaked shirt, and Liza immediately pulled her foot away.

"Let him look, baby," Jefferson crooned. "I've got you."

Sara put her arm around L. C. to comfort him and watched Ling work. "Tell me what happened," she said calmly but shakily to the boys.

'We were wading . . . there must have been some glass on the bottom . . . we didn't see it . . ." L. C. gasped out the story between dry sobs.

Amy arrived with the bag. Sara noticed Harrison standing on the bank watching, his face lined with worry.

"You're going to be all right," Ling said. "See, the bleeding has almost stopped."

Liza leaned over to see for herself. "It hurts," she said suspiciously.

"I imagine it does," Ling agreed. "You're being very brave. Perhaps Jefferson would carry you back to the house, and we'll see about getting it all cleaned up and properly wrapped. Would that be okay?"

Liza nodded. Then she looked at Sara. "Does this mean I get to stay home from school?"

"School's not until Monday—we'll see."

"You could take care of me and Harry together." Liza

was watching Harry come up the path behind them. "We could read stories," she added, clearly idolizing the tall stranger.

"Sounds like a splendid idea," Harry chimed in.

Sara gave him a look that was filled with exasperation.

He shrugged and grinned. "Hey, what can I say? I've always been a charmer where the young ones are concerned. It's the *Moms* I seem to have trouble with."

SEVEN

The week flew by, and with each day Harrison became stronger and a more intricate part of the household. When Sara had come down the morning following the aborted picnic, she had found Liza and Harry in the kitchen preparing breakfast.

By midweek he started walking with the kids to the highway when they left for school. "Good exercise for my leg." He lifted the cane that had replaced the crutches.

During the day he worked on the Reynolds case, spending hours on the phone or at Sara's desk making notes, doing research. A couple of times he had ridden into town with Ling to use the copier and fax machine at the local newspaper office.

He helped with the chores—not asking what he could do, but observing the needs and then assuming the tasks he could handle. When he wasn't working on the case, he would sometimes accompany Ling on his rounds or spend his time taking long walks alone through the woods that surrounded the farm.

With Sara he was easy and friendly. He put no pressure on her to continue what had begun at the picnic. He did not pry any further into the reasons for her choice of lifestyle; rather he showed interest in her work, examining the weavings closely and marveling over their beauty and intricacy.

In such an atmosphere, Sara was less defensive. She relaxed. They became friends, sharing news of their day as they sat with Ling after supper sipping coffee around the kitchen table or iced tea out on the porch.

"I've got an idea," Harrison announced Saturday night when the kids began to grumble that they were bored as they all sat around the kitchen table eating dessert. "Tomorrow, why don't we all go into town and see a movie?"

The eyes of the children swiveled as one pair to Sara.

"There is no movie theater closer than an hour's drive," Sara said.

All eyes went to Harrison.

"So, what's an hour's drive?"

Eyes right to Sara who seemed inordinately interested in her pie.

Liza broke the silence. "We have Sunday School and church, don't we, Mama?"

"We do have church," Sara said, continuing to eat her pie without seeming to acknowledge their silent pleas. "And then there's homework—it's always heavier on the weekends."

"I could do mine tonight," Jefferson volunteered.

"Me, too." That from L. C.

Sara looked at the boys. "All of it?"

Both heads nodded solemnly.

"Of course, there's Liza's foot. . . ." Sara's gaze shifted to the little girl.

"I'll carry her," Jefferson volunteered again.

"Besides, it's almost all better," Liza added. This from the same child who had been limping around, playing the small cut to the hilt all week. "See, I can stand on it real good." She hopped off her chair to demonstrate.

"Well . . ." Sara looked at each child in turn without

smiling. Then she said, "Okay," and went back to eating her pie.

When their whoops of joy died down, Sara reminded them of their promise to get their homework done.

"I'm afraid I, too, have a problem," Ling said.

"Yes, Ling?"

"I . . . uh . . . that is, the Reverend Thompson . . . that is, Amy asked me to join them for Sunday dinner after church."

"Ling has a girlfriend . . . Ling has a girlfriend . . ." L. C. sang and Liza picked it up immediately.

"Hey, way to go, dude," Jefferson added with a grin.

"Children!" Sara reprimanded them with a frown. "That's very nice, Ling. Maybe next time . . ."

"Yeah, maybe next time you and *Amy* can come," L. C. teased, emphasizing Amy's name in a singsong voice. Then he glanced at Sara's stern face and added, "I've got homework," and bolted from the room.

"Me, too," Jefferson agreed and followed him.

Liza seemed on the verge of tears. "How come I don't got homework?"

"Here we go, little lady," Harrison said, lifting her onto his lap. "How about reading me a story tonight?"

She giggled. "I can't read those books. They're too hard."

"You can't? Well, I'll be. What were you doing the other night when I skipped that one page in *The Cat in the Hat*?"

"Mama says I have those books . . . mem . . . memoried."

"Memorized," Sara corrected as she and Ling cleared the table.

"Well, you certainly know your letters," Harrison noted. "You'll be reading in no time."

Liza nodded. "Then, I'll read you a story."

Sara noted the way Liza seemed to take it for granted that Harry was here to stay. She had fallen into that way of thinking herself this past week. But, Harry would leave. It was a good reason for keeping things light, for keeping her distance. It had started to become too natural to fantasize about what might happen between Harry and her, given time.

Later, when she came down from telling the children goodnight and Ling had retired to his cottage, she found Harry doing some strengthening exercises for his knee.

"I think it's almost healed," he said and took a few tenuous running steps. "I think I could start to do a little running in the morning . . . nothing strenuous, just a little light jogging."

"This week has made a big difference," Sara agreed. She smiled at him. Yes, Harry Hixon would be headed back to New York before much longer. "Jefferson was telling me he knows about fixing bikes." It had become increasingly clear that Ling's busy schedule and new social life allowed little time for repairing bikes.

"Jefferson?" Harry was definitely skeptical.

"He said maybe tomorrow we could stop by this shop he knows and get the parts you'll need."

He studied her for a long moment before making his next comment. "Sara, what in the world is Jefferson doing here anyway?"

Immediately she was defensive. "Meaning?"

"Meaning, the kid has done some juvenile time. My understanding is that he was in the process of stealing your purse when you got involved. You could have been hurt, you know."

"I could have been, but I wasn't." Her voice was dangerously calm. "What exactly do you suggest we do about children like Jefferson, Harry? Write them off? Decide that at the age of fourteen there isn't a chance in hell they'll ever be any different?"

"I just . . ."

She started to pace. "People who think like that really get to me. I mean, you're so quick to pass judgment but where are you when the crunch comes? Where are you when it comes to creating some solutions?"

She glared at him. He opened his mouth to answer, but she wasn't waiting for that.

"Yes, Jefferson is a troubled young boy. You probably don't even know the half of it. He had a knife you know." She got some satisfaction from his shocked expression at that tidbit of news. "He probably would have used it if he'd been pushed far enough. He was that desperate."

"Holy . . ."

"I can see in your mind that's all the more reason for me to keep my distance, not to become involved. Well, Mr. Hixon, out here in the backwoods, getting involved is what a lot of people are about. We find it reprehensible that our children should come to this—carrying knives and going to jail and putting garbage up their noses. . . ."

He was grinning which made her even more upset.

"What?"

"You're pretty damned cute when you get all riled up," he noted.

She looked as if she might actually strike him. "Are we having a serious conversation here or creating B-movie dialogue? I thought you were interested in Jefferson."

He got up then and came very close to her. "I am interested in you," he said softly, "more and more each day."

She turned away and fussed with her loom for a minute. He allowed her the time to get control. "You are misjudging Jefferson," she said quietly after a moment. "He needs our support and encouragement, not our verdict on his life to date. Now, what about the bike?" She turned then and faced him, and he noted that she looked like a mother protecting her cub.

"I don't know. Maybe I should just ship it back as is."

Sara busied herself with picking up some of the children's belongings. "Well, whatever you think. We can check on that tomorrow, too, or maybe that'll have to wait until Monday.''

He frowned. The evening had started off so well—relaxed and easy without some of the usual tension between them.

"Hey, I thought we were going to the movies tomorrow, not fixing bicycles and gathering shipping data.'' He was smiling at her, but his eyes were questioning.

"Right you are,'' she said with a heartiness she didn't feel. Why was it every time she thought of his leaving there was this void inside? "Well, goodnight, Harry. I'm really beat—think I'll take a hot bath and read myself to sleep. See you in the morning?''

"Yeah. Okay.''

Harrison watched her go up the stairs. He stood watching her as she moved along the balcony to each child's room. Jefferson wasn't asleep yet so she spent a few minutes with him, talking and laughing softly. Harry wondered what she said to him and thought about how natural she was with each child. When she came out and saw him standing there looking up at her, she smiled and gave a little wave before going into her own room and closing the door.

She certainly was in a strange mood, he thought. He had looked forward to an evening with just the two of them. The children all off in their rooms . . . Ling out in his place . . . the fire to take the chill off the spring night. He glanced at the clock on the mantel. It was just past nine-thirty.

Harrison was restless and certainly not yet ready for bed. He sat watching the fire for awhile, thinking over the events of the day. He heard her come out and move down the hall to the bathroom. He heard the water running and the occasional splash she made as she moved in the tub, but she stayed there for a long time. Finally he decided maybe she was embarrassed to come out as long as he was sitting there, so he decided not to wait until morning for his trial run.

She was the damnedest woman, he thought, as he jogged along the gravel road to test his knee. One part of her was all brusque bravado and snappy comebacks. But there was another side that bordered on . . . shyness. No, more like skittish. There was a softer more vulnerable side of her . . . something that hinted at a history where everything had not always gone as planned.

Before he knew it he had run almost to the end of the drive, and his knee throbbed. He would pay for this tomorrow. He had put too much stress on the injury . . . gotten sidetracked thinking of Sara. Now he would have to start again with the regimen of rest and inactivity. He chuckled when he realized that idea was not so bad. It would give him an excuse to spend more time here.

He limped slowly back to the house and had just gotten to his room when the crying started. At first it was distant, like a cat mewing in the yard. But then there were shrieks, screams of pure terror and pain. He headed for the stairs without a thought for his reinjured leg. Using the banister as his crutch, he heaved himself up the stairs as fast as possible.

The doors to both Sara's and Liza's room were open. The cries, more subdued now, came from Liza's room. He remembered what Sara had told him about the nightmares.

He was breathing hard by the time he reached Liza's room and looked inside. Sara was sitting on the bed, the girl cradled in her arms. Sara was crooning words of comfort and Liza's sobs were beginning to trail off into shudders of dry air.

"The nightmare?" he asked.

Sara nodded and continued rocking the child. "Would you like some warm milk?" she crooned, and the child made a sound of assent, still clinging fiercely to Sara.

Harrison eased further into the room and sat down on the bed next to them.

Liza's eyes immediately focused on him. He had never seen such naked terror.

"Hi, kid. Bad dream?" Automatically he assumed the same gentle soothing tones Sara used.

Liza nodded, the wide dark eyes still riveted on him.

"Well, now, maybe we could all have a cup of hot chocolate. How does that sound?"

She nodded again.

"Maybe Mama could carry you downstairs while I go make the chocolate?"

Liza eased her grip on Sara slightly and turned so she could see him better.

"And then we could all three sit down there and have our chocolate—just like camping out."

The child nodded again.

"Okay, then. I'll meet you downstairs." Harrison found that it was normal to move in the same slow calm way he had been talking. He heard Sara continuing to comfort the girl as he left the room and made his way back down the stairs.

In the kitchen he put milk in the mugs to heat in the microwave. Rummaging around in the cabinets he found a box of instant cocoa and added spoonfuls to each mug as soon as the milk was hot. Hooking his fingers through the handle he was able to carry two mugs in one hand and the third in the other.

"Here we go," he said falling back into that mollifying tone that seemed to be effective with Liza. "There," he said as he handed Liza her cocoa and joined them on the sofa. "How's that?"

Liza sipped her chocolate and watched him over the rim of the mug. When Sara set the cup down for her, the little girl took the opportunity to scramble into Harrison's lap where she pressed close against him until he set his own cup down and folded his arms around her. With a sigh of pure contentment, the little girl put her thumb in her mouth and her head against his shoulder. "Tell me a story, Harry," she murmured.

Harrison glanced at Sara over the top of Liza's head. He felt completely out of his league. Reading books was one thing, but he wasn't exactly the world's champion storyteller.

Sara smiled at him. He noticed how different she looked, her hair free and falling over her shoulders, the chenille robe gaping just enough to reveal something lacy beneath. The moonlight played over her face, casting enticing shadows.

"Harry?" Liza's sleepy voice was still insistent.

"Okay, once upon a time . . ." He looked at Sara for help, but he knew from the wicked grin she gave him and the way she had settled back against the pillows that she would be no help at all.

"Once upon a time . . ." Liza prompted.

"Once upon a time, there was a beautiful princess named Liza." Small giggle from the diminutive form in his arms. "Liza lived in a magic kingdom in a valley at the foot of a mountain. She lived with the good Queen Sara who loved her very much. Liza was so happy there, because besides Queen Sara there were lots of friends for her to have. There were the good knights of Queen Sara's kingdom: Sir L. C. and Sir Jefferson and Ling, the Duke of Doctors."

"And Harry," Liza said softly and relaxed more deeply into his arms.

"And Harry," Harrison agreed registering Sara's look of surprise when he allowed the nickname to stand. "And Liza was very happy there. Even though bad things had happened to her before she came to the magic kingdom, she knew that here she was safe. Nothing could hurt her here. The good Queen Sara wouldn't allow that. So Liza grew up there and one day a handsome prince came riding on his beautiful white horse down the side of the mountain. And he said to Queen Sara, 'I have come for the beautiful Princess Liza.' 'Will you take very good care of her,' Queen Sara asked sternly. 'Oh yes,' said the prince. 'I will love her.' ''

Harrison looked at Sara. For a moment their eyes locked. His focus shifted to her lips which were moist and softly parted. He could think of little else besides kissing her.

''And the beautiful Queen Sara,'' he said huskily, leaning almost imperceptibly toward her, ''who was very shrewd and knew a good prince when she saw one . . .'' His voice had dropped almost to a whisper. His eyes had riveted once again on Sara's.

She blinked and moved to pick up her mug of hot chocolate, positioning it as a sort of shield between them. ''Liza's asleep,'' she whispered and then sipped the cocoa.

Harrison looked down and saw that she was right. Liza was sleeping peacefully, her thumb locked in her mouth, her breathing deep and steady.

''She'll be all right now,'' Sara said moving to take the girl from him. ''Thanks.''

''Wait a minute.'' Rather than hand over the child, he stood up and laid her carefully on the sofa, covering her tenderly with one of Sara's woven throws. ''Come here,'' he said offering Sara both his hands.

Sara looked startled but put her hands in his and stood up in compliance with his slight tug on her.

''I'd ask you to dance,'' he said softly, ''but I just came from exercising and I'm not exactly dressed for the occasion.'' He pulled her closer until she was standing just under his chin.

''And there's no music,'' she added.

''Ah, Sara,'' he said and pulled her into a full-fledged hug, ''must you be so damned practical all the time?'' He felt her tense at the contact of their bodies and held her firmly. ''Relax,'' he whispered. ''I just want to hold you.''

Gradually he felt her resistance slip. ''That's better,''

he whispered against her hair and continued to hold her, rocking slightly side to side as he did.

Sara had not thought of him as being so tall. So often, these past few days he had been sitting or lying in bed. But here he was a full head taller than she was. That was rare—Sara was a tall woman. Most of the men she knew were her height or even shorter. Those were her first sensations when she stood up and he took her in his arms.

But such attention to practicalities quickly dissolved into thoughts that were far more erotic in nature. She registered the muscular hardness of him, his chest against hers, the width of his shoulders, the arms that held her tenderly, loosely even, but with a strength and purpose that seemed incontestable.

She felt awkward and girlish just standing there so she put her arms around his waist, resting her palms against his back. He was wearing a t-shirt and sweatpants. She could feel the warmth of his skin through the thin shirt.

He was kissing her hair—light, flicking kisses that reminded her of a butterfly moving through her flower garden in July. She smiled at the image and ducked her head.

His finger caught her chin and raised her face to his. "I'm going to kiss you now, Sara," he said with great seriousness.

Sara's giggle was remarkably like Liza's. "Do you always announce yourself in such a solemn manner?" she whispered.

He smiled then. "Is that a yes?" he asked as his finger played over the shape of her mouth.

"Are you asking permission?" There was no trace of girlish giggle in her voice now.

"Not really," he said just before his mouth covered hers.

Of course, for Sara it was not their first kiss. She remembered vividly the way his lips fit against hers, the way his hands moved through her hair, caressing her head, pulling her closer. She had thought about that first kiss a

lot and at the oddest moments. And now here he was . . .
and it was better, because he was fully cognizant of kissing her.

She received him with a spirit and willingness that was
surprising to Harrison. He had expected reticence, even
resistance, but certainly not this. Her mouth under his was
compliant, receptive, even surrendering. This was not a
simple case of him kissing her—she was kissing him as
well.

He tested the boundaries by opening his mouth and
when she matched him, he was lost. It had been a long
time. Not that there hadn't been other women—lawyers
mostly or fix-ups from Nancy—but he had been just going
through the motions, hoping to get lucky maybe. No one
had elicited a response like this. He heard the rasp of his
breath as he kissed her throat, her ears, her closed eyes,
and then again that mouth.

Together they had unleashed a passion that neither
would have thought possible. His hands moved over her
shoulders to the opening of the robe, and that's when she
pulled firmly away. "No," she whispered and pulled the
robe tightly into place.

The only sound beyond her fierce "no," was their rag-
ged breathing. He touched her face, tenderly cupping his
hand against her cheek, marveling at the texture of her
skin, savoring the taste of her that stayed on his lips and
tongue.

"I have to take Liza up," she said moving away toward
the sleeping child.

He analyzed the tone and found no anger or regret there.

"Let her sleep," he said. "I'll watch her. I'll be right
here." He indicated the light from the sunroom.

"You need your rest," Sara said, but she did not move
to lift Liza.

"I won't sleep much tonight," he said, coming behind
her, but sensing he should not touch her. "I promise I'll

check her every few minutes. Come on, Sara, she's sound asleep. Don't run the risk of waking her.''

"Okay, if you're sure." She moved around the end of the couch and straightened the child's cover. With the protection of the sofa between them she risked a look at him. "I'll say goodnight then.''

He grinned. "So formal," he teased but saw immediately that the person standing before him was the vulnerable Sara. "Well, see you in the morning." He turned and bent to scatter the last of the embers.

"Goodnight, Harry," she said softly from the top of the stairs. "Be sure you check her—regularly, okay?''

"Goodnight, Sara," he replied and smiled because this was the other Sara, the one who took no nonsense.

In the end he had little choice but to go to church with them. Sara made it clear at breakfast that there were certain rules of the house and attendance at church was one of them. She had let him off the hook the week before because of his injuries, "but anyone who can run can walk into a church," she reasoned.

"I don't have anything decent to wear," he said after she had told him in no uncertain terms that they all had to set an example for the children.

"You have a perfectly nice pair of slacks and a shirt.''

He considered that as he watched her prepare the breakfast. It was true. He had thrown them into his knapsack at the last minute thinking perhaps he might want to spend a night or two in a hotel and might need something more presentable to wear than sweats or biking gear.

"They're wrinkled," he offered hopefully.

"Not anymore. While you were shaving, I ironed them." She went to a hook behind the pantry door and produced the freshly ironed clothes on hangers ready for wear. "I'll just put these in your room," she said and could not suppress a grin. "Children," she called as she moved through the house, "breakfast.''

By ten they were on their way. The church was a picture postcard rendition of what the songwriter must have had in mind in composing "Church in the Wildwood." It sat back from the side of the road in a clearing next to a pine forest. The building was frame, painted white with dark green shutters. The windows were a sort of frosted glass—not stained, but in their way more fitting to the setting.

Thompson's sermon played on the "Love thy neighbor" theme, and Harrison was favorably impressed with the global definition the minister chose to give the message. He sat next to Sara and was glad of the large attendance that forced close quarters in the small wooden pews.

After the service he noticed Sara talking seriously to the minister and a young woman he had not met. From time to time they all glanced toward the van, and Harrison could not decide whether the discussion was serious, judging from Sara's slight frown.

"What was that all about?" he asked as she came toward the van.

"Later," she said softly and climbed into the driver's seat. "Okay, let's get this show on the road," she said cheerfully.

At Harrison's insistence they stopped for burgers, fries, and malts at a local drive-in before heading for the movies. Disney films were not exactly his usual choice in movie fare, but with Liza in tow it was the only choice. Jefferson labeled it a "dumb kid's movie" while standing in line for tickets, but a tub of buttered popcorn had put him in a more receptive frame of mind, and they all settled in for the afternoon in the almost empty theater.

Sitting next to Sara, Harrison thought a lot about the night before. He was very aware of her—had been all day from the moment she had come down the stairs after breakfast wearing a dress. He'd never seen her in a dress. She even had on high heels and make-up. She looked great, not that she didn't always but this was special.

He thought about holding her hand in the movie, but

her attention was focused on the children, particularly Liza, who sat between them and asked a lot of questions as the movie progressed. Finally, his need for contact with her became so intense that he did something he hadn't done since junior high school. He raised his arms, stretched and allowed his arm to settle along the back of Liza's chair. From there it was easy to touch Sara's shoulder, her hair—which she had pulled back in a clip for the day—her neck.

She ignored the shoulder and hair part, but her face jerked toward his when he began a lazy massage of her neck. He pretended intense interest in what was happening on screen, and Liza asked another question.

For the rest of the movie, he had his way. He knew Sara could not really stop him without making a scene. So, following the massage of the back of her neck he allowed one finger to trace the outline of her ear, stroke her temple, and move down to her neck again.

At one point she looked directly at him until he was forced to meet her gaze. "I want you," he mouthed, which had the effect of her immediately shifting her eyes straight ahead once again to the screen. When he touched her cheek, he felt the heat of a blush. Still, she did not stop him. He found the place in the side of her neck where her pulse raced and left his fingers there for some time.

He began to fantasize about making love to her in front of the fire, on the porch under the stars, by the creek on a warm afternoon, in the big willow bed in her room.

"Wasn't that wonderful?" Liza was tugging at his sleeve as the credits rolled and people got up to leave.

"Yeah," he said and surprised himself with the huskiness of his voice. He looked at Sara. "Pretty wonderful."

Sara met his look for an instant and then busied herself supervising the gathering of jackets and caps and belongings. "That wasn't so bad now, was it, boys?"

"It was okay," Jefferson said grudgingly. "When do we eat?"

They moved through the lobby and out to the street. It was already getting dark, and the change in light surprised them.

"How about pizza?" Harrison suggested to the enthusiastic approval of the children.

"Pizza and hamburgers in one day?" Sara feigned disapproval.

"My treat," Harrison prodded.

"Not very healthy," Sara persisted.

"Ah, Mama," the three children said in a chorus.

Sara focused on Jefferson who had never called her Mama before. She looked as if she might cry.

"Well, Mama?" Harrison had caught the emotion of the moment and decided he needed to intervene, since clearly Jefferson had no idea what had happened that might make Sara cry.

"Okay, I'm outnumbered," she said with a smile.

The children whooped and raced ahead toward the pizza place.

"So, are you going to tell me what's going on?" Harrison asked as they walked toward the restaurant.

"Jefferson's mother wants him back."

EIGHT

There was no time to say more until after they had eaten and Harry had sent the children off with enough money to play video games for half an hour.

"Okay, what's the deal?" he said when he and Sara were alone.

She took a sip of her coffee and studied him for a moment. This whole day they had been like a family—mother, father, children. She realized how incredibly good Harry was with the kids—easy going and fun when possible but strict and firm when the moment called for it. Like when Liza had protested playing the games.

"I want to stay here with you and Mama," she had whined.

Sara had recognized the symptoms of an overtired child. She had glanced at Harry expecting to see him tuning out once the children stopped idolizing him and doing everything he said without question. L. C. and Jefferson stood by, waiting to see how things would turn out.

"Now, listen up, Liza," Harry had said, pulling the little girl onto his lap and bringing his face to her level so that she could see how serious he was. "There are some times when it's time for kids and other times when it's time for grown-ups. There are even some times when it's time for both. Like this afternoon at the movies—that was a time for everybody.''

Liza had nodded solemnly. L. C. and Jefferson had listened closely.

"This," Harry continued, "is one of those just-grown-ups times, which means you and the boys need to find something else to do. If we were home, you could play outside or work on your homework. But we're here, so I'm giving Jefferson some money and he's going to take you and L. C. to play video games, okay?''

Liza had looked from Harry to Jefferson and back again. "So, is Jefferson the babysitter, like when Mama goes out?''

"Yes. And when Mama goes out and you stay with a babysitter, you have to mind the sitter, right?''

Again the solemn nod.

Then Harry set her down on the floor next to Jefferson. "Okay, then Jefferson's in charge." He fished in his pocket and pulled out several quarters and added a couple of single bills to the pile. "Here you go, Jefferson.''

The older boy had actually given Harry one of his rare smiles and had then assumed the role of babysitter as if he had just been selected President of the United States.

"Sara?''

She blinked, realizing that she had been lost in thought and had stirred her coffee excessively. "That woman I saw at church?''

Harry nodded.

"That's Diane James. She's the county social worker. She got word yesterday from Charlotte that Jefferson's mom is moving in with her mother—Jefferson's grandmother—and they want him to come live with them, and Diane thinks it's a good idea.''

"Didn't you tell me there was some kind of drug thing there?''

"Drugs, alcohol. She couldn't pay her rent, so they

were evicted. I think Jefferson went after me because they needed money so badly. I don't want to send him back to that."

Harry had never seen Sara look so miserable. He reached across and took her hand. "I'm sorry," he said.

They sat quietly for a moment.

"It's just that . . . I mean, I always know there's the likelihood the children will move on—go back home or find a permanent family—it's just in this case . . ."

"Hey, it's not a done deal. I mean, maybe you can prove this woman isn't ready—what's it been? A few weeks? You don't just kick drugs and alcohol like that." He snapped his fingers to make the point.

It felt good to have someone to share this with, someone on her side. So often when one of her "kids" left she would cover her pain under a mask of proficiency and wit.

"You know, we were beginning to make a difference in that boy's life," she said after a moment.

Harry caught the unconscious use of the plural pronoun and hoped that she was including him in the statement. The pleasure he felt at that idea was surprising.

Then Sara shook her head sadly and went back to stirring her coffee. "Of course, with the grandmother in the picture, maybe . . ."

"Where has this grandmother been all this time?"

He echoed Sara's thoughts exactly. "I'm not sure. There wasn't a lot of time to talk after church. Diane will tell me more tomorrow. She seems to think the grandmother can make a big difference."

"When are you going to tell Jefferson?"

"Tomorrow—when I have some more details." She glanced toward the arcade where the children were laughing and playing. "I just wish I could have had more time."

"You've given him something he can hold onto, Sara," Harry said, reaching across the narrow booth to stroke the side of her face. "You give them all something they'll carry for the rest of their lives. Jefferson won't forget you.''

Later, after the children were in bed and Harry was returning a call to his law partner, Sara stood for a long time at the sink, doing the dishes they had left soaking after breakfast.

"Why don't you just put them in the dishwasher?"

She hadn't heard Harry come in.

"Sometimes when I need to think something through I like doing them by hand."

"Then I'll help." He picked up a towel and started wiping the glasses.

"Harry . . ."

"Just ignore me. You wash and think. I'll dry and keep quiet, okay?"

"Okay," she agreed with a smile.

But she didn't think about Jefferson as much as she thought about Harrison Hixon. He was different than she had thought he would be. The moment she had read ''New York'' she had assumed arrogance, and in those first hours of consciousness following the accident, arrogance was what she had seen.

Lately though, it was different, as if the two of them had sparred and danced around each other until they each thought they understood the other. Things were easier, more comfortable between them these past few days.

When his back was to her, she watched him wiping the dishes and putting them away. He knew the kitchen, she realized. He was at home here. She thought about the times they had shared since he'd come—the meals, getting Ling's place ready, church today . . . the whole day in fact. How easily they had made conversation, no long strained pauses, no embarrassment.

He turned suddenly, caught her studying him and smiled. It was a sexy grin that came from his mouth and his eyes. "Through thinking?" he asked as he folded the towel and hung it over the dish rack.

Sara felt herself blushing—it was as if he had read her thoughts. And in that particular moment her thoughts had had to do with how very good looking he was, what a nice body he had, and what it might be like to touch his skin, feel it against her own. She did miss that—a man in her life.

She scrubbed the sink with cleanser. "Thanks for drying," she murmured, assuming he would go back to his room and his work.

Instead he walked over and stood at the screen door. "Beautiful night," he noted.

Sara rinsed the sink and wiped the counters. In midwipe he came behind her, took the dishcloth and tossed it in the general direction of the sink and then with his arm around her led her toward the back door.

"Let's take a walk."

"The kids . . ."

". . . are in bed and Ling is watching TV right there in the living room." He turned and shouted. "Ling? Sara and I are going for a walk. Hold down the fort."

"Okay," Ling called back.

"See? Everything taken care of." He reached to open the door for her and bowed as he waited for her to walk through it.

"It's late," she protested, but walked out onto the porch and into the yard.

"In New York it's early yet. At nine o'clock there, things are just beginning to heat up."

"You must miss all that . . . the action and excitement."

He shrugged. "I'm not much of a party animal. I do enjoy a play now and then, and the restaurants are incredible. And you would go crazy over the museums and galleries."

"I'd like to visit sometime."

"Good." He draped one arm over her shoulder and

steered her toward the path that led to the main road. "I want you to visit—often."

Now he was being courteous, she decided. Time to make some gesture of appreciation for her hospitality. As if to prove her point, he said, "I've really appreciated being here, Sara."

"I'm glad. It's been good for the children meeting you, you know. You're very good with the children. I'm sorry you and Catherine . . ." She stopped, shocked at the presumption she was making to speak of his dead wife, to reopen his pain.

"Catherine didn't want children." The way he said it was almost as if he was speaking to himself, as if he had forgotten that fact and was surprised to remember it.

"And you?"

He glanced at her, then smiled and pulled her closer under the wing of his arm. "I want children. Now, do I at last get to ask you personal questions since you have opened the subject?"

"Such as?"

"You know what the questions are. Why haven't you ever married? Why does a beautiful, intelligent woman choose to bury herself on the side of a mountain instead of being out where some lucky guy can find her? Come on, Sara, give. Inquiring minds want to know."

"It's not exactly checkout line headlines. I just never met the right guy—time passed." She shrugged as if to end the subject.

They walked in silence for several minutes. "What about Bo?"

She didn't look at him. "What about Bo?"

"Amos mentioned him." Harry waited, but she said nothing. "Well?" he prompted.

"Well," she replied somewhat testily, "he was somebody I once . . ."

"Loved? Almost married?"

"Amos has a very big mouth," she muttered.

"Amos likes you, as do a lot of people. They also worry about you. They ask the same question I did earlier—what's a woman like you doing hiding out . . ."

"I'm not hiding. I grew up here." She stopped, shrugging out of his casual hold on her. "I think we'd better start back." She turned and started walking back toward the lights of the farmhouse.

"I think," he said, grabbing her and pulling her tight against his chest, "that it's time you gave me some straight answers. After all, you know about me, about Catherine. Come on, turnabout's fair and all that."

She looked at him, trying to decide whether to trust him. What did she know about him anyway? He was a stranger who had dropped unexpectedly into her life. But in the few days he had been there something had happened between them . . . a bonding, a growing respect. It had been a long time since she had shared anything personal with another adult. But for some reason she didn't fully understand, she decided to share this with Harry Hixon.

"Bo and I were engaged . . . sort of. In this part of the country, folks would say we had an *understanding*. He was the local high school football coach. He came here the year after my folks died. I had inherited the farm, and he needed a place to stay, I rented him the cottage."

"Where Ling is?"

She nodded.

"No wonder it didn't need all that much work. When was this?"

"Four or five years ago. What does it matter?" She pulled away again and started walking, but this time she headed away from the house. "Well," she said when she had taken several steps and he was still standing, "do you want to hear this or not?"

"Coming."

"So he was around and we started . . . seeing each other, going to church together, out after the games. . . ."

"The town must have been all abuzz," Harry noted.

She gave him a silencing look and then walking and looking down at her feet she continued. "After a year of that he gave me a ring. We started making plans. It was textbook classic formula romance."

"Sounds boring." At her look, he added a contrite "Sorry."

"I had a couple of kids living here then. I'd just started that. Also I was just beginning to make a name with my weaving. I had won two major show awards and a commission for a commercial piece in Charlotte. Then Bo got an offer to coach at a small college near Chicago. The athletic director there was an old college roommate. Bo had just signed a new contract here, but this was a chance to move into the college ranks, and, he jumped at it. I guess he thought I would, too."

"Why didn't you?"

"I had trouble with loyalty. This was the middle of the season. The coach at the college had quit suddenly and they wanted him right away. I thought he should have said that he'd be thrilled to come as soon as the season here was over. It seemed to me that this town had been very good to him and that perhaps he owed them that, even if he didn't stick out his new contract."

"But he left?"

"Yeah."

"Didn't he ask you to come?"

"Oh, sure, but he wanted me to drop everything the way he had. I'm not like that. I had the kids and the commission. I had responsibilities." She was quiet for a long moment, then added. "Bo couldn't understand that."

"And later?"

"Later never came. He left angry at me, and I was angry at him. I wrote trying to smooth things out, but he didn't understand why he didn't come first . . . not just first, but way ahead of whatever might be second. He couldn't understand why I wouldn't just about sell my soul to escape this place, move out into the larger, more exciting world. He called a couple of times, and then came the letter that he'd met someone else . . . someone he'd known in college. They'd been pretty much of an item, I guess. He used to talk about her when he was here. Oh, he had told me that was in the past, but sometimes the way her name would come up.'' Sara shrugged as if trying to bring herself back from those memories. ''So, I sent back the ring and that was that.''

''What do you mean 'that was that'? That was five years ago—what about since?''

''In case you haven't noticed, the place is not exactly teeming with eligible bachelors, not to mention the fact that in those five years I've aged. I wasn't exactly a blushing ingenue when Bo was here.''

''Bull. There must be lots of guys. Besides, now you're branching out with your work. You want to tell me there hasn't been some art dealer or social worker or businessman who hasn't made a pass at you?''

''I've had the occasional date if that's what you're driving at.'' He was starting to get on her nerves, and she couldn't for the life of her figure out why she was allowing this conversation to continue.

''Well, if once in a while you'd let your hair down—literally—and get out of those infernal jeans, you might find it happening a lot more than just now and then.''

She faced him then, her fury welling up, her insecurities about her looks and the passing of time bubbling to the surface as well. ''In case it's slipped your notice, I work damned hard for what I have here. I don't have a lot of time for hairdressers and make-up, not to mention shopping for the latest fashions. I wear jeans because they don't get in my way. I put my hair up for the same reason. I look like this because it's easier and faster. It leaves a lot more time for me to take care of ungrateful, arrogant, shallow city slickers who decide to conquer major mountains on bicycles in the middle of an oncoming spring snowstorm.''

She would have said more but he kissed her then, passionately. One hand held her head to him as if in a vise; the other hand pressed her hips firmly against his own. "God, you're something else," he muttered when he allowed them both a breath before kissing her again.

At first she was so startled that she just stood there. Then she pressed both fists against his chest and pushed, but he held her tighter. Then her palms opened against his chest touching the hardness she had been fantasizing about back in the kitchen.

He released the clip that held her hair, and she heard the metal ting of it hitting the gravel road. Then both his hands moved from her neck to her hips and back, an erotic massage that soon expanded to circle around her ribcage to her breasts, which felt heavy and full to bursting, waiting for his hands on them.

Then his mouth was against her ear, his tongue tracing the outline of the lobe, and she was holding on, pulling him closer until she could feel the hammer of his heart against her own.

Other nights, when she had lain in her bed thinking of Harrison Hixon, she had promised herself she would not allow this. He would leave and where would she be? She couldn't go through that again.

"Sara, do you have any idea what having you come into my life at this particular moment has meant?" He was kissing her again—short kisses on her eyelids, her cheeks, her temples. And his hands were cupping her breasts, his thumbs stroking her nipples. "You did more than save me from physical disaster. Don't you know that? Don't you know what you give these children—what you give everyone whose life you touch?"

Her mind raced. So, what was this? Gratitude? She didn't want his gratitude. She wanted . . .

"We have to get back," she said, effectively shutting her mind to thoughts that could not be. Her voice came out in a whisper, even as her mouth reached for his again.

She allowed herself the rapture of the kiss before moving away. "We have to get back," she said again and started toward the house.

Harry caught up with her and took her hand. They did not speak again until they had reached the yard.

"I'll see to the animals," she said, and he let her go.

She stayed in the barn for some time, doing things that didn't need doing, busywork to keep herself from thinking about what had just happened.

By the time she went back to the house all the lights were out except the one over the sink in the kitchen and by the stairs in the living room. Ling had gone back to his cottage, and Harry had gone to bed.

Typical man, she thought with irritation and disappointment as she climbed the stairs. *She would probably be up all night thinking about this, and he was sleeping like a baby. Did it mean anything to him?* She felt betrayed as she had with Bo. She had allowed them to see her most private self, and they had taken it for granted. Had Harry been thinking of Catherine while he was kissing her tonight?

She saw the note when she turned on the bedside lamp. It was propped against her pillow with a tulip from the yard.

I'm not going to press, Sara. You need to deal with the Jefferson thing now. But when that's all sorted out, I will be there. I'm not Bo.

The next morning was easier than she would have thought. That was because Harry was acting as if things were as normal as ever. It also had to do with the fact that Diane James showed up almost as soon as the kids had left for school. Harry sat with Sara while Diane explained the situation.

Jefferson's grandparents lived in Charleston. Somehow their daughter had been able to keep them at bay with assurances that all was well. From time to time they had sent her money, and the one time a year she visited them with Jefferson, she had answered their concerns about how thin and haggard she looked with further assurances that she was just tired. It was only when Jefferson's grandmother came to Charlotte for a surprise visit a week ago that she grasped the full reality of the situation.

"She's a wonderful and caring woman, Sara," Diane assured her. "I'm convinced that what she says is true. She never knew."

"That's impossible," Harry objected. "How could she not know?"

Diane gave him a sympathetic look. "I understand how upsetting this all is. But you need to understand that Jefferson's mother in spite of all her problems is able to do whatever is needed for her own survival. It's perfectly within the realm of possibility that she was able to put on a good enough act to fool her own family . . . especially with them hundreds of miles away and unable to afford to visit more than once a year."

Harry looked at Sara to see how she was taking all this. She was being very quiet. "Sara?"

"I'm sure Diane's right." She looked at the social worker and smiled wearily. "After all, it's not the first time we've seen a kid's parents fool everybody, is it?"

Diane looked at her friend with resignation. "No, and it surely won't be the last. I'm sorry, Sara. I know how you feel about Jefferson, but I really do think the grandparents can make a real difference, and he should be with his family if it's at all possible."

"I'm sure you're right," Sara agreed.

After Diane left, Harry stayed with Sara. She didn't seem inclined to discuss the matter now that the decision had been made, but he hoped his presence gave her some comfort. When a call came from Greg in New York, she insisted that she would be fine and that he should concentrate on his work.

The rest of the day he spent working or making calls.

The Reynolds case was heating up he explained that night as they sat with Ling over coffee after supper. He needed to prepare some papers and get them into town to the fax machine by the end of the week.

"I have to talk to Jefferson," Sara said excusing herself from the table.

Harry got up too. "I'll go with you."

Ling stopped as well. "Me, too."

Tears welled as she considered these two different men who had come into her life at the same time and already were such a part of her family. "Thanks, but maybe for this I'd better talk to him alone."

The two men nodded but remained standing.

"When we tell Liza and L. C., though," Harry said just as Sara turned to go upstairs, "I think we should all be there . . . do it as a family."

Ling nodded.

Sara just shook her head and smiled, coming back to each of them for a hug. "Thanks, guys. Don't think I can't see that you're trying to make this easier." Then without looking back she ran up the stairs.

Jefferson took the news in silence and without looking at her. But when she hugged him, he did not resist and even hugged her back for an instant.

By Wednesday they had told Liza and L. C. The arrival of Jefferson's mother and grandmother had been set for Sunday afternoon, which, of course, meant the time for Jefferson's departure had also been set for Sunday.

In spite of the pall of intense sadness that hung over the house that week, there were moments Sara knew she would cherish forever: like the afternoon Amos showed up unexpectedly and asked if he might borrow Jefferson to help him on some of his rounds, and the suggestion from Ling and Amy that a surprise party be planned for him for Saturday night in the church fellowship hall.

But the memory she knew would stay with her forever was the morning she came downstairs and found Jefferson

DETACH AND MAIL CARD TODAY –

FIRST CLASS MAIL

PLACE
POSTAGE
STAMP
HERE

OFFICIAL ENTRY CARD

Kismet Romances
"$1,000,000+ Sweepstakes"
PO Box 7249
PHILA PA 19101-9895

and Harry sitting on the step of the back porch talking. Neither of them heard her so she listened shamelessly from the kitchen.

"You know, when I first saw you . . ." Harry was saying.

"You thought, 'Uh oh, black kid, must be trouble,' " Jefferson finished and there was an edge of challenge in his tone.

Harry grinned. "Yep, exactly." Then he added more seriously, "But, I was wrong, Jefferson. Unfortunately you're going to run into that a lot. It's not right, it's not fair, but it's reality. It's the way it is out there."

"Tell me something I don't already know, man."

"I'll tell you this. You changed my mind, and you can change anybody else's too. I mean that. You've got a choice. It's a hard choice, but still a choice. You can be pissed off all your life at the unfairness of the world—and with good cause—"

"Or?" Jefferson actually looked at Harry for the first time.

"You can make up your mind who you are, get comfortable with that, and not let anybody take it away from you."

"Easy talk," Jefferson muttered.

"Yeah, it is. It's going to be damned hard for you, Jefferson. But you've got a couple of things going for you."

Jefferson looked interested and listened.

"You're smart—not just streetwise, but intelligent. And you've got a family that wants you."

"Wants the welfare check, more likely."

Harrison reached over and touched the boy's shoulder. "Don't judge until you give them a chance, Jefferson. If you're right you'll know soon enough, but don't make it hard for them to love you. Love doesn't come along that often in a person's life."

"So, what else I got going for me besides my big brains?"

"You've got Sara. She'll always be here for you—at the other end of a phone, at the other end of a letter, whenever she comes to Charlotte. You can count on this lady, Jefferson. You can take what she's given you and bank on it to always be there for you. Do you understand?"

"Sort of. She's okay."

Sara smiled as she brushed away a tear. "She's okay," was high praise from Jefferson.

"And one more thing." Harry reached into his pocket and pulled out his wallet. He handed Jefferson a card. "You've got yourself a New York lawyer, kid. Now, get this straight, I won't bail you out of your own messes, but if you need help I'll be there for you, okay? If things don't work out at home or you get in something that's over your head, give me a call . . . collect. Oh yeah, and keep your grades up and I'll see what I can do about finding you some money for college."

"You shittin' me?" Jefferson took the card and grinned at Harry.

"Strictly business, okay?"

"Yeah, man, okay."

They gave each other some sort of ritual handshake that Sara was surprised to see Harry knew, then set off together to do the morning chores.

After school an atypical quiet pervaded the house. Harry was on the phone, Ling was off doctoring the Haines twins, and the three children were nowhere to be seen. Sara went looking for them.

She found them in the barn clustered around Jefferson who was working on Harry's bike.

"What's up?" she asked.

Liza, as usual, assumed her role of spokesperson. "Jefferson's gonna fix Harry's bike. It's a surprise. We're helping."

As if to underline that last, L. C. handed Jefferson a pliers.

"I'm gonna need some things," Jefferson muttered in her general direction.

"Ling could get them for you tomorrow while you're in school. Make a list. I'll see he gets it."

The children put in an appearance for supper, then raced back to the barn, Liza almost giving it away by giggling and eyeing Harry throughout the meal.

"What's going on?" Harry asked.

"Secrets," Sara said and finished clearing the table. "How's the case going?"

"You're changing the subject."

"And you're dying to talk about this Reynolds case with somebody," she teased.

He frowned and leaned back in his chair. "It's the damnedest case," he said and then spent the next hour filling her in on all the intricacies of the biggest case he had ever had.

"Winning this could be very important for you, couldn't it?" she observed when he had finally run down.

"It's important for the firm, and on top of that we're on the right side here."

"Aren't you always?"

He was quiet a minute. "We try to be. Sometimes it's hard to tell."

"And that bothers you?"

He sighed. "Sometimes you take a case because you need the money for the firm to keep going. You take it, and you hope it turns out right. In the Reynolds case we could make enough money to pick and choose the cases we wanted for a long time to come."

"And on top of that your side is right."

He nodded. "That's the nice thing about this one—if we win, we win big time."

"Then I hope you win, Harry," she said, getting up from the table.

Harrison watched her moving around the kitchen, calling the children in from outside, packing lunches for the following morning. He noted that she had not worn her hair up in a bun since that night. She still pulled it back at the nape of her neck with a clip, but she hadn't put it up once. And she wore her shirts tucked into her jeans or pulled up and tied at the waist, not hanging out concealing her body as she had before.

"Want to take a walk?" he suggested and knew that she was clear on what he was asking.

She hesitated, then busied herself putting the lunchbags in the refrigerator. "Can't tonight, I'm afraid. I really need to get some weaving finished and Jefferson needs some help with his math homework and . . ."

She turned and he was there. His arms went around her and his face was very close. "You got my note?"

She nodded. She was backed up against the refrigerator. There was no escaping the presence of Harrison Hixon. She thought he must be equally formidable in the courtroom.

"Good. Then we understand each other. You go do your weaving, and I'll tackle the math homework." He pulled her to him and kissed her just as the screen door banged open.

"Whoa," Jefferson said with a wide grin.

"Radical," L. C. added. It was his latest word, and he used it for any occasion he considered worthy of comment.

"You kissed Mama," Liza chimed in noting the obvious. "Does that mean you all are gonna get married?" She seemed hopeful.

"It means, little lady, that I like your Mama a whole bunch," Harrison said moving to pick Liza up and hoist her to his shoulders. "Now isn't it about your bedtime?"

The kids followed Harry from the room, but not before L. C. had glanced back at Sara and repeated, "Radical, Mom," with a grin and a wink.

NINE

On Friday Harry went to town with Ling. The newspaper editor, Ed Bower had offered him the use of his office, phone, and fax machine for the day, and Harry had gratefully accepted.

The children were in school, and Sara was weaving when she heard the car on the gravel drive around two. Folks in the area tended to leave their doors open and be casual about dropping in, so Sara assumed whoever had driven up would come in through the kitchen and find her. That's why she was surprised to hear footsteps on the front porch. Coming to the front door meant something official.

Her immediate thought was the kids—one of them was hurt on the playground perhaps. Then as she hurried toward the door, she thought of Ling and Harry. Perhaps an accident, she thought as she opened the front door.

There were two black women standing on the porch, and Sara knew at once that they were Jefferson's mother and grandmother. The reality of the teen pregnancy issue hit her square in the eyes as she considered her guests. One was in her late twenties at best and the other was not yet fifty. Jefferson was fourteen.

"Hello," she said holding the screen open with her hip

and offering her hand in greeting. "You must be Jefferson's family."

The grandmother accepted her handshake and smiled. "I'm Odessa Preston. This is my daughter—Jefferson's mother—Maella."

"Maella, it's a pleasure to meet you." Sara offered her hand, and it was accepted in a limp handshake and with no eye contact.

When she had offered the women tea or soda and been refused, Sara took a seat across from them. "Jefferson's in school. He'll be home in about an hour. He's been doing really well in school—gets good grades on his homework and on a test last week he scored in the eighties." She was babbling and knew it.

Odessa gave her a sad smile. "This is hard for you. We understand that," she said softly.

Maella looked at Sara for the first time and gave a little nod. "Thank you, ma'am," she said in a high-pitched child's voice, "for what you done for Jefferson."

"Why don't you ask us the questions on your mind, honey," Odessa said.

The questions on her mind—Sara almost laughed at that. There were a hundred questions. Why were they here two days early? Where were Diane James and the social worker from Charlotte? What were their plans?

"Are you moving to Charlotte, Odessa?"

"No, Maella and Jefferson will live with me."

The magnitude of that information struck Sara like a blow. "In Charleston," she managed.

Odessa nodded.

They sat for a minute, the ticking of the grandfather clock the only sound.

"So, Jefferson will be . . ."

"Living with us in Charleston, Sara," Odessa repeated. "I'm a teacher there. I have a good job. Maella's father and I think Maella can . . . heal better there, and Jefferson can have a fresh start. There are some good children there—young people he can be friends with.'' She was making her case—one mother to another.

Sara nodded and got up. If she didn't physically do something she was going to scream. She wished Harry were there—he was good at this. He had charmed the socks off everybody in town. "I'm going to get us some lemonade. I just remembered I made a pitcher this morning."

In the kitchen she put both hands on the sink and braced her whole weight against it while she closed her eyes and fought back tears. She had thought she had come to grips with Jefferson's leaving. She had told herself it wouldn't be so bad. More and more she did shows in and around Charlotte, and she had thought she could persuade his family to let him come visit, too—a weekend, a week. . . .

Like a robot she made up the tray—glasses, pitcher of lemonade, napkins, plate of cookies. She went back to the living room.

"You have a lovely home," Odessa said as she accepted the lemonade and selected a cookie.

"Thank you. Jefferson has his own room. Would you like to see it?"

Now Odessa and Maella seemed happy to have some physical action to pass the time, too, so the three women trooped up the stairs, the lemonade and cookies left barely touched. Sara was showing them some of his school work and artwork when she heard the second car on the gravel. *Harry,* she thought with relief. But again, there were steps on the front porch, and she heard Diane James call her name.

"Excuse me," she said and hurried down the steps to meet the social worker.

"Diane, what's going on?" she asked as she stepped out onto the porch. She lowered her voice, knowing Odessa and Maella were not far behind.

"Sara, this is David Miller."

The heavyset man who stood just behind Diane moved around her to offer his hand. "Ma'am," he said, nodding his greeting.

Sara shook his hand but turned her attention back to Diane. "Something's happened," she guessed.

Diane turned to David. "Dave, would you mind giving me a few minutes with Sara?"

"Okay if I wait inside?" he asked Sara.

"Fine." She was brusque and she knew it, but she didn't like surprises and the appearance of every one of these people on this particular afternoon was a definite surprise. "Okay, what?"

Diane sighed and sat down in a rocker, indicating that Sara should sit down as well. "First of all, I'm sorry Jefferson's family got here before us. I got held up at the office just as we were leaving. I didn't know Dave had sent them ahead. He didn't know I hadn't had a chance to talk to you yet."

Sara gritted her teeth and gripped the arms of the rocker. "Just spit it out, Diane."

"Odessa needs to be back in Charleston tomorrow—her father-in-law has had a heart attack."

"So, why don't we just postpone this? Why can't she go back, take Maella along, and come later for Jefferson?"

"It's expensive enough for her as it is, Sara."

"But she could use the time to get Maella straightened out, help her in-laws. . . ."

"Sara, no. You know how these things work. It's not going to be that way," Diane said gently.

Sara looked at her for a moment, felt the tears building and swallowed them back. "He's going today?"

Diane nodded and patted her hand. "I'm sorry, Sara."

"Excuse me." Odessa was standing at the screen door. "I wonder if Sara and I might have a moment?"

Diane looked at Sara who nodded, and then she went into the house as Odessa took her place in the rocker.

"Sara? I'm so sorry about this—that it's happening like this," she began.

Sara kept her eyes focused on her hands. "Don't you think you need some time? Diane tells me there's sickness in the family . . . and there's Maella. . . ."

"I understand your feelings. It just seems to me that if we're going to be a family, we need to just jump in there and get started."

Sara risked a look at the older woman's face. "I could bring Jefferson down. I know it's expensive . . ."

"It isn't the money. I really think this is the way to do this. It's time Maella and Jefferson saw that there is a working family here with pain and pleasure and all the things that go with being a family . . . like you've shown Jefferson here."

They rocked in silence for a moment.

"You know, Odessa, when you take in kids like I do, you always know they aren't yours . . . not really. . . ."

Odessa chuckled, a soft low rich sound that Sara found likeable. "Honey, they aren't yours even when they are yours . . . not for keeps anyway."

Sara smiled and nodded. "Yeah, well, with Jefferson, I guess I feel I need some more time. We're just getting used to each other."

"Oh, Sara, we don't want you out of Jefferson's life. I'm hoping you'll visit and that he'll visit you."

"I'd like that. You know, he was a big help on a fair I did a few weeks ago, and I'm going to miss his help here with the chores and all . . . not that I've expected him to do chores. . . ."

"Well, I hope you have expected that—it's good for him. What about this? If everything goes okay these next few months, what if Jefferson spent say July or August here?"

"That would be wonderful."

"And maybe you and the little ones could come down to Charleston one weekend . . . Mother's Day, maybe."

Sara looked directly at Odessa. This was a good, nurturing, loving woman. She had thought this out; she had seen all sides. She was trying hard to make the best of a terrible situation. "Thank you, Odessa," she said softly and stood up.

"No, honey. Thank you." Odessa stood up and hugged Sara. "You know I'm well aware that without you, my grandson might be in jail right now and my daughter would never have gotten the help she needed. We thank you, Sara."

That's how Jefferson first saw them—his grandmother and Sara hugging on the front porch. He was walking up the road with L. C. and Liza from the school bus. Liza spotted them first. "Mama," she called, "who's that?" Then she and L. C. took off running toward the house.

Jefferson hung back and saw Sara explain to the younger children and send them off to play. Then she stood there waiting with his grandmother.

"Jefferson," Sara said when he was close enough so that she could speak in a normal voice, "there's been a change in plans." He noticed how her voice was funny even though she was smiling at him.

"Hullo, Granma," he muttered.

"Don't I get a hug?" Odessa said and walked down into the yard to meet him. "Your mama's inside." She put her arm around him and led him up the stairs and into the house. Sara held the screen door for them.

The rest of the afternoon flew by and yet seemed to move in slow motion. Sara and Maella packed Jefferson's things. The mother was young and certainly fragile, but maybe it would work, Sara told herself. At Odessa's suggestion they drafted a letter of agreement about visits and calls and letters.

"This is a contract," she explained to Jefferson. "It says what we grown-ups are going to do. Read it and see what you want to add."

That's when Ling and Harry returned, coming in

through the back door, talking about the day and stopping suddenly as they entered the living room and saw the gathering before them.

"I'll have my lawyer check it out," Jefferson said handing the paper to Harry.

Introductions and explanations were made. Harry looked over the letter, glancing frequently at Sara to get a reading on her feelings, her mood.

"I'd like you to all stay for supper," Sara said when Harry had advised Jefferson to accept the letter as a gesture of good intentions on everybody's part. "It can be an early one," she added, knowing they were anxious to start back.

"We have to eat," Jefferson threw in as if he couldn't care less, but his eyes focused pleadingly on his grandmother.

"Good point," she said and got up. "Sara, what can I help you with?"

In the end it was like a party—the one they'd planned for Jefferson the next day at church. Amy Thompson came by, and two of Jefferson's friends from school were with her. Later Sara would find out that this wasn't an accident—Ling had called Amy as soon as he had heard about the change in plans.

"We had just stopped by Mrs. Haines's house to pick up the cake for tomorrow," she said. "Might as well have it tonight."

"There should be presents," Liza had announced.

"We'll send the presents," Amy promised.

Finally, when everything was packed, including the left-over cake for them to eat on the trip, everyone moved to the front porch. The time for leaving had arrived.

"Now, honey, you remember what we promised," Odessa said as she hugged Sara again.

"Mother's Day," Sara agreed. Then she turned to Maella and held out her arms for a hug.

The young woman hesitated, then fell into Sara's arms,

tears rolling down her cheeks. "Thank you, Sara," she whispered. "I just wish . . ."

"You just take good care of our boy," Sara said, fighting back tears of her own.

Then she turned to Jefferson and handed him one of her woven throws. "Put this on your bed in your room, okay?"

Jefferson nodded mutely, his eyes fixed on the soft colorful blanket. "Got to do one thing," he muttered and took off around the side of the house, handing the throw to Odessa as he went.

L. C. and Liza raced after him, and the adults waited in puzzled silence. In a moment the three children came around the house, Jefferson pushing Harry's repaired bike.

"Jefferson fixed your bike," L. C. and Liza screamed in unison, their faces alight with the delight of having actually kept the secret.

Everyone was smiling—even Maella who walked out into the yard and put her arm around her son's shoulders. "You did this?" she asked in wonder. "I'm so proud."

Harry tried the bike out and pronounced it better than new. Then he took Jefferson aside while the others looked on curiously.

"Harry says I can take the bike," Jefferson announced as if he hardly believed the news himself. "It's mine . . . to keep."

"*If*," Harry prompted.

"Oh yeah, if I mind Granma and keep up my grades."

"You heard the deal, Mrs. Preston," Harry said turning to Odessa. "If the grades fall . . . or the discipline . . . the bike gets taken."

"You're too generous, Mr. Hixon. We'll see that Jefferson appreciates your gift."

The bike was strapped onto the loaded car, and in what was suddenly too short a time, Odessa, Maella, and Jefferson started to get into the car.

"Jefferson," Sara said softly, not knowing how she planned to finish.

He was halfway in the front seat already, but he came back and hugged her hard. "I won't forget, Mama," he whispered and then without another look ran back to the car.

The motor was already running. Odessa pulled away waving as she went.

Soon after, the others left as well—first the social workers, then Amy with Jefferson's friends. Ling went with them.

L. C. and Liza seemed a little stunned by the events of the day, so Sara spent a long time putting them to bed, answering their questions, easing their minds. In some ways it was therapeutic for her as well.

Harry stopped in to tell them each goodnight, promising to take them fishing in the creek the following morning.

"Do you want to be alone for a while?" he asked as they closed the doors to the children's rooms and started downstairs.

"I'm not sure," she answered and smiled because it was the most honest answer she knew. "It's been one hell of a day."

"Might help to talk it through," he noted. "I made some tea while you were getting the kids down."

"That sounds nice."

They sat in the kitchen, and she recounted the events of the day. "It seems like it was a long time ago that I heard that car come into the yard," she said when she had finished.

They heard Ling come home. He stuck his head in the back door to see that Sara was all right and to say goodnight.

Harry was glad for Ling's presence on the place. Given the news he had gotten from New York this afternoon, Ling would be a big help. He listened to her talk about

Jefferson, saw the tears well, and said, "Let them come, Sara."

He watched her struggle against revealing that much emotion to him and lose. The tears came first in large plopping drops that hit the table, her mug of tea, and the back of her hand. Then came the steady downpour. "Jefferson was different—more challenging than the others. We were just beginning to connect. I miss him already," she whispered.

Harry moved his chair closer, rubbed her back, offered his handkerchief. Then he pulled her to her feet and stood there holding her until the crying was spent. "Better?"

She nodded and blew her nose. "Yeah. Thanks."

"You know what I think you need?" He didn't wait for an answer but started walking with her toward the stairs. "I think a good hot shower and a good night's sleep would make you feel a lot better about things in the morning."

"Maybe."

"No maybes about it. Come on. You go get your things. I'll start the water running so the bathroom will be all steamed up when you're ready, okay?"

It did seem like the best idea, so she agreed. She went to her room and undressed. When she came out a few minutes later, the shower was running and Harry was downstairs watching television.

She stood under the shower for a long time. She allowed herself one more crying jag and then decided that was enough. Time to move on. She believed Odessa Preston to be a woman of her word. Jefferson was still going to be a part of Sara's life, just not living here.

When she came out, the downstairs lights were out except for the light coming from Harry's room. She thought about going down to tell him goodnight, but knew she was thinking about more than a simple goodnight. No, it was better to just go on to bed.

In her room she saw that he had come back up while

she was in the shower. Her bed was turned down and on the nightstand was an old canning jar filled with fresh spring flowers from the yard. Next to it, a note,

Sleep well. See you tomorrow bright and early. I don't know a damned thing about fishing and desperately need your help.

Harry

She laughed out loud at the note and went to bed smiling. Just before she went to sleep she realized she'd never asked him about his day, about what Greg had had to say from New York about the Reynolds case.

On Saturday the kids were up with the birds, impatient for Harry to come through on his promise. When he stumbled in for breakfast, he looked less than rested.

"Coffee?" Sara brought the pot to the table and poured him a mugful.

"Just leave the pot," he muttered.

"Harry, what kind of fish are we gonna catch?"

"Harry, do you think there's any real big ones?"

"Harry, what kind of bait should we use?"

"Harry, does fly fishing mean fishing for flies?"

"No, stupid. When you fly fish, you use flies for bait. Isn't that right, Harry?"

The children seemed to be taking turns interrogating him.

"Children, give Harry a chance to eat his breakfast. Now the first thing you're going to need is some bait—worms. Go out to the garden and fill up that empty margarine cup over there, and put the lid on it. When you've done that we'll be ready."

"Thanks," Harry said when they had gone.

"Consider it a debt paid for last night." She refilled his mug and set a plate of bran muffins next to it. "Thanks for the flowers, Harry, and the note."

"Oh good, then you know how much trouble I'm in with this fishing thing." He grinned and wolfed down the first muffin.

He ate as he had since the first meal she had offered him—with gusto. It was a pleasure to cook for someone so appreciative.

"Got the worms," L. C. shouted through the screened door.

Sara instructed him on where to find the poles and tackle box, and the four of them set off for the creek. The children either did not notice or did not comment on the fact that Sara was clearly running the show, instructing them on everything from where on the creek to go, to baiting the hooks, to not tangling their line. Harry learned along with them.

"I got one," he shouted soon after dropping his line in the water for the first time.

Certainly the pole was bent almost double.

"Wow," L. C. exclaimed, his eyes wide with awe.

Sara smiled. "Well, reel him in," she said and waited.

Harry tugged and tugged, but nothing happened.

"Must be humongous," L. C. said.

"Oh, it's humongous all right," Sara said, no longer able to contain her laughter.

Harry looked over his shoulder and frowned. "You think you can do better?" He offered her the pole.

"You've caught your line on something," she said as she took the pole. "This is more likely a rock or some weeds than a fish." She wiggled the pole and line around trying to free them, but in the end she cut the line with a pair of nailclippers she had Liza get her from the tackle box. She handed the pole back to Harry. "Back to square one," she said and handed him a hook and a worm.

They spent the whole day with the children. After fishing, they went back to the house and packed a picnic for lunch. Then they drove over to Amos's farm and went horseback riding. Amos and his wife invited them to stay for supper, and they accepted.

When they got back to the house, the phone was ringing. It was Odessa. "How you doing, honey?" she asked when Sara picked up the phone.

"I'm okay. How's everything there?"

"Not bad. I think Jefferson was expecting the worst, so whatever we came up with was better. As I told you he has his own room, and a neighbor came over earlier—a boy he'll be in school with. They spent the day together—riding bikes, shooting basketball. How's Harry and the kids?"

Sara told Odessa about their day. She liked the woman more each time they spoke.

"You gonna marry that man or let him get away?"

Sara smiled. "I'd say that's for him to decide, Odessa."

"No, honey, that's for *you* to decide and do something about. They don't come along too often as good as that man . . . not to mention as good-looking. Whoo-ee, that man has got one great set of buns, honey."

Sara actually blushed. Harry was sitting not ten feet away sharing a bedtime snack of milk and cookies with the kids.

"I'll tell him you said hello," Sara said.

Odessa laughed at that. "Don't waste your time delivering messages from an old woman like me. You get those kids in bed, and then get that man out there on that porch swing under that full moon and see what you can develop."

"Goodnight, Odessa. Give Jefferson our love and tell him I'll call next weekend."

She hung up and realized they were already establishing a pattern, a routine of staying in touch. It made her feel better.

"Come on, kids. Time for bed. Church tomorrow. Come on, scoot."

She felt happy as she helped Liza undress and get into bed, as she went down the hall to L. C.'s room and tucked him in, as she moved back down the stairs and saw Ling and Amy sitting close together on the porch . . . in the swing . . . in the moonlight. Harry was sitting in the rocker across from them.

She thought about the call from Odessa, about what the woman had said about Harry. She thought about how nothing in life is for keeps—you take what you get—like she had had Jefferson for these few weeks, something she would hold on to forever. And even though he would leave eventually, Harry was here now. What was wrong with enjoying the time they had? What was wrong with storing up some wonderful memories?

Outside, she exchanged banalities about their day with Ling and Army, then turned to Harry.

He was in a strange mood. Gone was the happy-go-lucky good humor of the day. Now he seemed pensive, introverted, even upset. He glanced at her and then immediately focused on the darkness.

"Nice night," he commented.

When he suggested they go for a walk, she agreed. Ling and Amy were there to check on the children should they need anything. "They'll probably sleep like logs—they had a very active day," she said.

"Take your time," Amy said. "We're not going anywhere." Then she looked up at Ling with eyes full of love.

There was enough of a moon to light the path, and

they walked in silence until they came to the small bridge that spanned the creek and led into the pine forest beyond. When Harry put his arm around her shoulders as they walked, she did not move away. The sound of the water spilling over the rocks was soothing, reassuring—a sound she had grown up with. And everywhere they were surrounded by the perfume of the night—the pines, the loamy soil, the wildflowers that had burst into bloom in the week of warm weather.

"Let's sit out here for a while," he said after they had crossed the bridge and were walking along the bank under the pines.

They sat, she with her chin resting on her knees, watching the occasional leaf that floated by in the creek. He lounged next to her, putting his weight on one elbow. She felt him watching her and, finally deciding he was still concerned about her emotional state now that Jefferson was gone, said, "I'll be all right," more to reassure him than anything else.

"I have to go back to New York," he said softly.

She thought the comment incongruous to the current situation until it registered that he meant immediately. It was a blow.

"The Reynolds case?"

"Yeah. Sara?"

She felt him move closer but remained as she was, arms tightly gripping her knees, eyes focused on the water. "When?"

"Tomorrow. They moved the court date up—the other side. It's to their advantage not to let this thing play out too long. We have to be in court on Tuesday."

TEN

In the weeks to come Sara would reflect, from a purely practical point of view, on the decision she made that night on that bank by her creek. Harry had been the most intelligent, witty, and attractive man to pass through her life in years. Further, it was likely to be years again before she met anyone else so engaging. It might never happen again.

Ever since the fiasco with Bo—long before Harrison Zachery Hixon, Jr., came into her life—Sara had come to an understanding about what her life would be. She would live on her mountain, doing her art, raising the kids who came and went, and, if she was lucky, occasionally finding someone interesting to spend time with. These were choices she had made over time. She had good friends and a satisfying and active social life built around her art and the community. She felt luckier than most and spent little time dwelling on the fact that at her age and in her circumstances the likelihood of finding Prince Charming held two possibilities: slim and nonexistent.

So after Harry was gone back to New York, she thought of that night a lot, but she willed herself to think of it without regret—no maudlin sighing over what might have been. They had both known the score going in. Just because it had been perhaps the most wonderful night of her life, just because she couldn't stop thinking about him, just because every little thing reminded her of him . . .

It occurred to her that she'd done more crying recently than she usually did in a whole year. She had cried that night, the tears coming naturally as soon as the word "tomorrow" was out of his mouth. Since he had left, she could close her eyes and remember every detail of the rest of that night. Sometimes she didn't even have to close her eyes.

"I don't want to go, Sara," he had said quietly. He had moved very close to her. If she turned her head, their faces would have been close enough to kiss. "Sara?"

"Well, you have to." She tried to give her voice that let's-get-on-with-it tone she often used to hide her own emotions, the tone she had used with Jefferson, the tone she had used in explaining why Jefferson had to leave to Liza and L. C., the tone she had used with herself after Jefferson was gone.

"Look at me," Harry demanded roughly, and his hand turned her face to his. He saw the tears. For a moment his expression registered surprise, then tenderness, as he gently reached with one finger to stop the flow.

He kissed her then, slowly, thoroughly, tenderly. If he had been demanding, if he had strong-armed her into submission, she would have been able to rekindle her earlier determination not to allow him to touch her life any more than he already had, but his gentleness and compassion were her undoing. The tears came freely now, bathing both their faces as the kiss deepened and the passion she had resisted found its release in her need not to miss the chance to know him completely.

"Sara." He whispered her name again and again as his mouth moved over her face.

Then he started to unbutton her shirt, his eyes moving from the work of his fingers to her face to see her reaction, waiting for her to stop him. When the last button was undone, he pushed the shirt off her shoulders.

She heard the intake of his breath and realized that to him in that moment she was desirable.

"Sara, I want to make love to you. . . ."

"But?" She had caught the inflection in his voice. It made her nervous, which made her wisecracking self-defense mechanism automatically kick in. She pulled her shirt closed.

"But," he said softly, smiling as he traced the outline of her breast with his finger, "I don't want there to be any regrets. Any way you look at it, I leave tomorrow."

"I know." She relaxed her grip on her shirt, and he once again pushed it off her shoulders, leaning in to kiss her neck as he did.

"So," he said huskily as he continued to move his mouth and hands over her shoulders, neck, back, and breasts, "at some point we're going to have to stop this and go back to the house and get up tomorrow and say goodbye." He undid the clasp on her bra and moved to fondle and kiss her there.

"I don't want to say goodbye yet," she said, with a low moan for punctuation when his mouth closed over one nipple. They had found their way to the ground, and she could feel the softness of the pine needles against her back. She could also feel the power of his arousal on her thigh.

"We have time," he whispered as he moved back to kiss her again.

They stayed that way for what seemed on the one hand like hours, on the other like seconds, kissing and touching. Gradually their clothes came off—his t-shirt so that his rough hair-covered chest finally touched her smooth silky one. Then jeans were unbuttoned, unzipped, pushed away. Underwear became the last barrier.

They touched and tasted. At one point he reached into the creek and allowed the cool water to drip from his hand onto her chest and stomach; then he sucked away the droplets. She searched out all the places where his pulse pounded against the heat of his skin and kissed him there, allowing her tongue and teeth to tease him unmercifully until he was groaning with agony and ecstasy.

He grinned and stood up. ''Come on, lady, it's cool down time.'' He offered her his hand. ''Come on. A wade in the creek should do the trick—in the absence of a cold shower.'' He was laughing, but she could see that he was painfully aroused, that he was as ready as she was.

For an answer, she removed her underpants and lay back. ''Please, Harry. Let's make this our place . . . our night.'' She held up her hand to him.

''You're sure about this?'' Clearly he wanted her. ''No regrets in the morning?''

''No regrets, Harry.''

He finished undressing, put on a condom, and sank to his knees, pulling her to him. ''Be very sure, Sara,'' he said huskily just before his open mouth found hers.

She was sure. She knew what she was doing. She knew the rules. She knew that he would leave, that she would stay—alone again, at least in this sense. She knew that after tomorrow she and Harry at best would exchange an occasional phone call or letter, that Christmas cards might come for a few years, that in time he would go back to his real life and tonight would be just a memory. It would be enough, she decided and fit her body to his before either of them could change their minds.

Afterwards they lay on the cool soft ground for a long time, holding each other but not speaking, each lost in private thoughts. She wanted to ask him about Catherine but knew that wanting to hear him talk about his wife meant wanting to hear him say that Sara had eased that pain, had opened his heart, had taken Catherine's place. She knew that asking him anything about his life was asking him to make her some small part of it, and she wouldn't do that.

"Will you drive me to the airport?"

"What time?"

"Tomorrow night. The flight leaves at six." Then, as if reading her thoughts he added, "Ling and Amy said they would watch the kids."

"It's going to be so hard on them . . . especially Liza. She's in love with you, you know." Sara smiled at him and wondered why he frowned back at her.

"How about this idea? How about if we take them, make an afternoon of it, go to Charlotte, tour the airport, have dinner. . . ."

"Harry, they'll be okay. They're tough. You don't have to—"

"I want to. I'm going to miss them. Hell, have Ling and Amy come along too."

She giggled at that. "Don't you want to include Amos and maybe the Thompsons? How about the crew down at the newspaper?" With each addition to the list she tickled him.

"All right, enough," he replied and grinned down at her. Then his eyes went serious, and she knew he was going to kiss her.

"I'm going to find it hard to leave the kids," he said when the kiss had turned sad and desperate and she had broken it to avoid the pain. "But you . . . Sara, I'm not sure what's happened here on your mountain, but . . ."

She placed one finger against his lips to silence him. She didn't want their night spoiled by his feeling he had to set things right by saying things he didn't mean or wouldn't mean in a week.

"I like you, too," she whispered with a smile she hoped was convincing.

"Good. Would you care to show me how much?" His smile was devilish and sexy and irresistible.

As wonderful as that night was, the following day was very tense. In the end she decided the children should stay at home with Ling and Amy. They had school the next day, and there was too much emotion for them to deal with already. The day passed slowly, one of those days where there's something important to do at the end of it and until then it's a process of marking time.

It was Harry who seemed to have regrets about their lovemaking the night before. He was withdrawn and silent most of the day, breaking out of his mood only to play with the children. He spent the morning helping Ling plow and prepare the vegetable garden. After that he started to pack and load his things into the van. At two he came to the kitchen.

"Any time you're ready," he said.

"Just give me a minute to write a note for Amy. She's coming by to fix supper for Ling and the kids."

Harry nodded. "I'll go tell the kids goodbye."

Within half an hour they were on the road, Harry driving, Sara silent beside him.

"Look," she announced finally when she could not stand the tension for one minute longer. "About last night."

He glanced at her and started to say something but she stopped him.

"Just let me say this, okay?"

He nodded and focused his attention on the road, but his knuckles whitened from the grip he had on the steering wheel.

"Harry, last night was very special to me." His grip relaxed, and some color flowed back to his fingers. "It's a time—this whole time of knowing you—I'll cherish. We've grown to be friends." That brought a glance that could only be described as surprised.

"We were a hell of a lot more than friends last night," he said.

"Yes. But that was last night and today is something else. You are leaving—going back to your real life—and we both have to deal with that. I mean who are we kidding here?''

"What are you getting at?" The grip was back.

Sara sighed searching for words. "I'm just trying to be practical, trying to hold onto what we can without messing it up with a lot of strings neither of us wants."

"Once more, in plain English, please."

Now she was getting frustrated. She usually had no trouble being direct. She wondered if she was having so much trouble now because she was delivering a very mixed message. "Okay, direct and to the point. We are not lovesick teenagers. We are grown-ups. The reality is that you have your life and I have mine, and the likelihood is that while we hopefully will stay in touch, as time goes by the . . . intense feelings we had for each other last night will . . . dim. The contact will be sporadic at best."

"It doesn't have to be," he said and smiled at her.

"Now you see, that's part of the fantasy. It's like what we've shared these last few weeks. It seems very authentic, very strong, but it isn't real. And if we try to maintain the masquerade, we're going to end up not being friends at all and I would really hate that, Harry."

"So, what are you suggesting?"

"I'm suggesting that we be adult about this and admit right here and now that there are no expectations . . . that I don't expect you to call me or write to me all the time. I mean, of course, I want to hear from you now and then but on a normal basis, not a forced one." God, she had never had so much effort finding the right words.

"I'm not to write or call?" He sounded angry.

"I didn't say that. I just said that it ought to be . . . unforced."

They rode in silence for some time. The tension was almost tangible.

"So, I take it visits are also out." Now his tone was bordering on sarcastic.

"Look, Harry, I'm just trying to put this in perspective.

Believe me in a week or so you're going to thank me for being so rational about all this.'' Her voice rose. She was shouting and gesturing.

By contrast he took a low and ominously calm tone. "I don't recall asking you to manage my feelings, Sara. But then maybe you're right. Maybe I read what's been growing between us all wrong. At any rate, please don't worry. I won't be harassing you with calls or letters.''

"You are determined to make this into a major deal, aren't you?'' Now she was terse, staring ahead, her arms folded tightly across her body.

"No, Sara, you've shown me it's no big deal.'' He pulled the van into the airport entrance and instead of heading for the parking area pulled up to the terminal.

Sara glanced at him. "Are you going to unload first?'' He didn't have that much stuff.

"No, I'm getting out. You're heading back. It'll be dark before long. I don't like you out on those mountain roads at night.'' He handed her the keys and got out.

She had little choice but to get out, too. "Well, I guess you're right,'' she said while she waited for him to get his luggage from the back.

He dropped the bag on the curb and turned to her. Then without a word he pulled her into his arms and kissed her. "Thank you, Sara Peters, for coming into my life, for rescuing a greenhorn, for sharing your home and your family . . . and most especially, for last night.'' Then he kissed her again and let her go, picking up his bag and heading for the automatic door.

"Let me know how the Reynolds case comes out,'' she called.

He half-turned and nodded and waved but did not break stride.

The kids were cranky the week after Harry left. Too many leavetakings, Sara decided, especially for children who had had to face losing family before. L. C. was particularly affected, arguing with Liza, talking back to Sara and Ling, and finally getting into a fight at school. His attitude did not improve with time, and Sara could not help noticing that whenever Harry's name came up, L. C.'s face clouded over and he either sulked or misbehaved.

Sara's days were filled with work she had too often neglected in favor of spending time with Harry and the children. The art fair season was coming on fast, and she didn't have nearly enough ready. Plus there had been a call from a gallery in California interested in her work.

That first week Harry did not call, and there were no letters. At the beginning of the second week there was a note saying how swamped he was, how badly things were going with the case, and asking about the kids. The third week there was a large box filled with Easter baskets, stuffed animals for Liza and L. C., and a straw gardening hat for Ling. There was also a book about wildflowers for Sara. She did not miss the careful impersonality of it.

That night she decided to call and thank him. She told herself that it was the polite thing to do and that this silence had gone far enough.

"Yeah," he answered the phone. He sounded hassled and distracted and exhausted.

"Harry?"

"Sara?"

"How are you?"

"I'm okay. What about you . . . and the kids?"

"Fine. We're all fine. They loved the Easter presents."

"Great. How's Ling?"

"Good. He got a kick out of the hat." This was impossible. It was like talking to a stranger. "Thanks for the book."

There was a pause. "I miss you," he said finally, and instantly it was more like the Harry she knew.

"Me, too," she answered.

They relaxed a bit then. He asked about her work and

wanted to hear all about Liza and L. C. She asked about the case.

"I have to be in L. A. next week," he said. "There's a guy who could blow this thing open for us if I can get him to come back and testify."

"There've been a couple of stories about the case in the paper here. It's really getting national attention."

"Yeah, Greg was on the news the other night."

"You sound tired."

"Yeah, it's been a grind, but things are starting to happen. Greg and I are starting to be cautiously optimistic."

Another pause.

"Well, I just wanted to thank you for the gifts—they were a nice surprise. Take care, Harry."

"Yeah. You, too."

The next day the florist delivered a crystal vase filled with multi-colored roses and baby's breath. The card read:

Thanks for calling—it made my day. Thanks for listening. Thanks for letting me know you're still there.
Harry

The week passed quickly. Sara found herself attacking her work with more energy and dealing with the children with more patience. She'd been right to set the guidelines for Harry's going back to New York. The tension that had existed at the airport was gone. "And there's no pressure to live up to anything because we let enough time pass so that everything got back to normal," she found herself explaining to Ling and Amy one night as they lingered over their iced tea after supper.

"Maybe you're right," Ling said politely, but the glance he sent Amy was skeptical.

"What?" Sara demanded, looking from one to the other.

"It's just that Amy . . ." Ling began.

"Ling and I thought you and Harry made a wonderful

couple. Everybody in the valley wants someone special for you, Sara. You're too extraordinary not to have everything life has to offer—including love.''

Sara smiled. Had she ever been that young? That much in love with love? Yes. She remembered how it felt, that first real love. ''You know, children, take it from an old lady of thirty-two, when you're young and in love you want to share that with everybody. You cannot stand to see anyone without a partner. It's not uncommon.''

''We're not talking about just matching people up willy-nilly,'' Amy said softly. ''We're talking about you and Harry.''

''Harry lives in New York. His work is there, his family is there, his friends are there, and his life is there. I live and work and have family here. Sometimes even when something seems so . . . possible, reality gets in the way.''

Amy frowned. Ling cleared his throat, and Sara stood up.

''Well, it's been a long day. I think I'll turn in. Goodnight, you two.''

She was surprised to hear the distinctive tunnel sound of long distance when the phone rang Sunday night.

''How's it going, Sara?''

''Tommy?''

''In the flesh—in the pink, too. How are you and who the hell is Harry?''

''What?''

''Harry—Hixon, I think, he said. Came by the clinic the other day to see me. Seems pretty sweet on you.''

Sara could not believe she was hearing this. ''Harry came to see you?''

''Hey, is this a bad connection or what? I just said that. Now what gives?''

''He's a friend.''

Tommy laughed and it was good to hear him sound so

normal—no booze or drugs in that laugh. "And I'm the ghost of Elvis. Give me a break, Sara. I'm all grown up these days. I can actually handle adult topics."

"Really, he's a friend. He spent some time here after an accident he had while on vacation. He lives in New York."

"Uh huh." Tommy sounded far from convinced. "Well, take it from this old cowboy, the man is hot for you."

"What did he want with you?" Not to mention how had he found Tommy, why had he bothered, how had he even remembered Tommy was in L.A.?

"Wanted to remind me that you gave me my start— that if it hadn't been for you I'd be digging ditches or in jail, the latter more likely."

This was bizarre. "What did you say?"

Tommy laughed. "I told him nobody knew what Sara Peters had done for me more than I did."

"And he said?"

"He said, 'You sure got a funny way of saying thank you getting all choked up and worrying her half to death, especially when she can't do anything to help you.' Damn, he was steamed. I thought he was gonna punch me."

"Tommy, you're making this up."

"How could I? It's too weird. I mean, the guy was all over me—verbally speaking. Told me I'd better stay clean or answer to him. So, what's the deal? You two getting married or what?"

"We're friends," she said again. "So, how are you?"

"Good, Sara." Suddenly he was serious. "I mean it—I think, maybe. I mean it's one day at a time, but so far . . ."

"I'm glad."

"And relieved?" He was teasing her again.

She laughed. "It's good to hear from you."

"So, tell me all the news. How are the kids? How many have you got these days?"

She filled him in about everything that had happened and was surprised to realize that it had already been two months since his call from the party—the night he had been drunk and drugged. "Tommy, can you come home?"

"I'll get there. I'm here for another month, then I need to go to Nashville for a recording session. I should be able to stop by from there. Want to make the wedding then?"

"Tommy," she said warningly.

"Oh yeah, you and Harry the He-man are 'just friends.' Give me a break, Sara—better yet, give Harry a break. The guy's nuts about you."

"Tommy, deal in reality. He's in New York. I'm here—not exactly an easy commute." She felt as if she should put that line on automatic playback, she was saying it so much lately.

"Hey, guess what? They've come up with this new thing—it's called moving. You go there; he comes to you. Get the picture?"

"Say goodnight, Tommy," Sara said laughing.

"Goodnight Tommy."

"I'm glad you're better. Now don't jump back into tours and recording sessions and all that too soon."

"Yes, Mother." Then once again he was serious. "Sara? I do appreciate it, you know . . . all the stuff you did for me. Harry's right. Without you . . ."

"It's never all one way, Tommy. Remember that. You give a lot back. You have a lot of love that goes beyond your talent."

"How about this? I'll write a song and sing it for the wedding."

"Tommy." He could be exasperating—even as a child he had been.

"Catch you later, Sara. Give a good report on me to Harry. I don't need him coming after me just when I've gotten all put back together again."

"Goodnight, Tommy. I've got to get some work done."

"Oh, wait, that reminds me. Did that chick from the gallery in San Diego call you?"

"That was you—the gallery showing?"

"Hey, you're the artist. I just acted as your agent."

"Thanks, Tommy." She was very touched.

They talked a minute longer and then hung up. Sara was smiling. Things weren't so bad. Tommy was better, Jefferson was doing very well, and even L. C.'s current phase of anger and mayhem would pass.

Harrison tapped his pencil against the desk.

"Earth to Harrison," Greg said, sticking his head around the door of his partner's office.

Motioning for Greg to come in, Harrison shuffled some files on his desk. "I was just thinking about that Los Angeles witness—how he really saved the day for us on this one."

"Yeah, it was a good win—a big one in lots of ways. We should celebrate."

"Good idea. Call Nancy and I'll make some reservations."

"Why don't you bring someone? It'll be more fun."

Harrison shrugged the idea off. "Too short notice," he said, reaching for the phone. "Besides we're the three musketeers, remember?"

It was something Nancy had started following Catherine's death—a way of letting Harry know they were there for him, that they would not press.

"I think we've sort of outgrown that," Greg said quietly. Then he grinned. "You know, you haven't even had a date since you got back. When are you going to admit to me that this woman on the farm in North Carolina was not the old hag you led me to believe she was and give me some real details? Nancy is driving me crazy. Come on, fella, my marriage is on the line if I don't bring her just one crumb of gossip."

Harrison continued to dial the restaurant, but did smile at his friend. "Okay. She isn't the old hag I led you to believe she was," he said.

"That's it? That's what you're going to give me?"

Harrison shrugged. "Take it or leave it."

"You aren't going to get off this easy. Nancy will carve you up for the main course at dinner."

Greg underestimated his wife's determination. They had barely sat down before she started. "So, tell me about this woman—Sara?"

Harrison glanced at Greg, then turned his attention to Nancy. "You'd like her. She's very straightforward like you."

"Good. Now if only you were. Come on, Harrison, give—age, weight, body type, hair color, eyes, personality."

"I can see we aren't going to get to eat if I don't talk, so listen carefully: Sara is tall—about five seven, I would guess." *She fits just under my chin when I hold her.* "She's slender. She keeps in shape running a farm and a business by herself I suspect." *She has this incredible body that fits next to mine like a glove.* "Her hair is kind of . . . it's long and straight and dark—maybe she has some Indian in her ancestry." *It's one of the sexiest things about her—a man could get lost in that hair, could be warmed by that hair, could . . .*

"Eyes?" Nancy seemed to mentally be taking notes.

"Smoky . . . like blue/gray . . ." Harrison thought for a moment. He wasn't doing her justice. He frowned. *Her eyes were so expressive—wide and challenging when she was confronted, soft and dewy when she made love. . . .*

"*Smoky* sounds very sensual," Nancy teased.

"She has a great laugh . . . a great sense of humor. . . ." Harrison almost seemed to be talking to himself now. He was smiling.

Greg nudged Nancy, and they both studied their friend and then rolled their eyes at each other.

"So, when do we get to meet her?"

Harrison came back to reality. "Probably not for a while."

Nancy was aghast. "You mean you haven't invited her here?"

"You have to understand. She raises foster children, she's a weaver heading into her peak earning time, and she has the farm, not to mention this student doctor living there."

"He's the one who treated you?"

Harrison grinned. "Well, yeah, with a little help from the local vet."

Now it was Greg who was astonished. "The *vet*? You never told me that. I assumed you'd at least been checked by a real doctor—someone credible."

"Ling Hu is very credible. He does good work." Suddenly his tone was curt, impatient.

Again Nancy and Greg exchanged a look. Harrison had changed—a lot.

"No wonder it took you so long to heal and get back here," Greg muttered as the waiter delivered the entrees.

"Actually I healed pretty fast considering the concussion and the knee thing and all. Nope, I just strung it out because I liked being there. It was all so different. I mean I actually took the kids fishing one day."

"You? Fishing? Like with one of those bamboo sticks and such?" Nancy was hearing more than even she could process.

"Well, the pole was a step above bamboo, but I did bait my own hook." He waited for their interested but puzzled looks. "Worms—we dug 'em in the garden. Actually, the kids did that part."

"My God, you sound like you enjoyed it," Greg said.

"I did. It was very relaxing . . . and fun. We had a lot of fun that day." He started to laugh and told them the story of his caught line. "Sara was so funny that day. She comes out with some of the best lines. . . . What is it?"

They were both staring at him as if he had just dropped in from Mars.

"It's you," Nancy said. "It's been so long since we've seen you like this—easy and happy and at peace with yourself."

"It's been a good week," Harrison said off-handedly and raised his glass. "Now let's get to this celebration business. To the Reynolds case—the one that put the firm of Hixon and Thomas in the spotlight."

ELEVEN

For most of the rest of the evening he and Greg discussed business—new cases coming in, which to take, which to refer elsewhere. Nancy, who normally took an active role in even business conversations, was uncharacteristically quiet.

"So you guys are getting away next week," Harrison said as they waited for a cab. "Where're you headed?"

Greg had opened his mouth to answer, but Nancy jumped in, "Hilton Head. Why don't you come with us?"

"Now there's your basic good idea," Greg added. "I mean, we've been working our buns off. Let's just get away for a week. Come on—some sun and sand, a little golf. What do you say?"

Harrison was tempted. Hilton Head was nice, especially at this time of year. Maybe he could talk Sara into meeting them there. Or he could fly down with Greg and Nancy, stay for a day or so of golf and tennis, and then rent a car and drive to Sara's. He could even stop in Charleston and see Jefferson. Still, there was the firm to be managed, and he had taken a great deal of time off already. This was a time for Nancy and Greg.

"Sounds great, but there's the office. Plus, if you recall, I just came back from a trip."

"Sylvia and the rest of the staff run the office as it is, and Jason and . . . what's that new girl's name?" Nancy turned to Greg.

"Her name is Connie, and she's a junior partner. I hardly think she would appreciate being called a girl unless, of course, you're going to refer to Jason as a boy."

"Okay, you made your point. The thing is you have a very capable staff, and they can certainly handle things for a week. Besides your trip was interrupted by your accident. It was more like sick leave than a vacation. Come with us, Harrison."

"Well, maybe . . ."

Nancy did not let him continue. "Great. I'll make all the plans. You two just be ready to leave in one week, okay?" She smiled brightly and kissed Harry's cheek. "Goodnight, hon, and congratulations on the big win."

Greg handed her into the cab and turned to shake hands. "It was damned good work, buddy," he said referring once again to the Reynolds victory.

"Get some rest—you've earned it." Harrison gave his partner and friend a brief hug. "See you," he called to Nancy as the cab pulled away.

"You want to clue me in on what that was all about," Greg said when he and Nancy were alone in the cab.

"What?"

"Don't play innocent, Nancy. You have a plan here and it involves Harrison and matchmaking. When are you going to learn?"

"I just thought we should stop by, say thanks for taking such good care of our friend, meet the lady . . ."

"You want to go to North Carolina?"

"Well, you can't exactly get to South Carolina without at least going close to the place."

"It's at the other end of the state, honey."

Nancy smiled and nodded, and Greg could see the wheels turning as she made plans.

"We are not doing this," he said firmly.

"Not even if I call and let her know? Not even if it's exactly what Harrison is dying to do himself?"

In court the man was known as a bulldog, but when it came to his wife and her incontestable sense of romance, Greg was defenseless. "We'll call . . . once." Nancy grinned triumphantly, but Greg held up his finger to make a point. "*And* if we get no answer, or if the lady is not home, we will not leave a message and we will not call again and we will *not* just stop in, understood?"

"Absolutely, honey," Nancy replied and turned her head to look out the window. "I'll call her in the morning."

Sara carried the phone closer to the loom. She often didn't bother to answer it when she needed to concentrate on a project. On those days she would sometimes bury the phone in the closet behind a pile of coats so it wouldn't distract her. Even now, she needed all her concentration to get this one piece finished for the gallery show, but since Easter she never wanted to take a chance on missing one of Harry's calls. The one telling her about the Reynolds win had come mid-morning, and they had stayed on the phone until noon.

She had chastised him for the expense, but in fact she had been delighted that he hadn't been able to wait to share the news with her.

Sara threw the shuttle and banged the beater against the threads, her feet working in rhythm to her thoughts as she recalled the conversation. So lost was she in daydreams of Harry that the phone rang three times before it registered with her.

"Sara?"

The voice was unfamiliar, but the accent implied New York. "Yes."

"Sara, this is Harrison's friend, Nancy Thomas. My husband, Greg, and Harrison are law partners."

"Of course. How are you?" *And why on earth are you calling? Has something happened to Harry? Is he hurt? Sick?*

"I know this sounds strange, but Greg and I are on our way to Hilton Head. We're flying, and I see that we change planes in Charlotte. Is that anywhere near you? I mean, I thought if we were going to be in that part of the country, perhaps we should take a day and see some of the area. Perhaps you could advise us on what to see and where to stay?"

"Oh. Well, of course, I'd be happy to help with what I can. When are you leaving?"

"Day after tomorrow. We get to Charlotte mid-morning. Is there enough to see that we might want to stay over a day or so?"

"It depends on how long you have. If you're anxious to get to Hilton Head . . ."

"Oh, that's just our destination—you know. Greg and I often take time along the way to taste the flavor of areas we've never seen."

Sara tried to form some impression of the woman on the other end. She sounded bright and interesting, but what she was proposing was pretty ridiculous. If she were talking about a longer vacation . . . still, it was her trip.

"Well, in this area you might enjoy taking a day and driving over to Asheville. The Vanderbilt estate is there, and that's always interesting. There's a wonderful old inn there, too."

"Is all that near you?"

"Well, not too far." Sara's suspicions were growing by the minute.

Nancy rushed on. "Because Harrison has talked of little else since he got back, and Greg and I would love to have you meet us for dinner. We'd like to express our gratitude for all you did for Harrison. My dear, it sounds to me as if you saved his life."

Sara smiled. She was pleased at the news that Harry had been talking about her with his friends. "Look, on your way to Asheville, you practically have to come right by my place. Why don't you stop here, have supper . . . and stay the night if you like?"

"What a lovely offer, Sara. Thank you. We should be there sometime the day after tomorrow. Why don't I call you when we get into Charlotte and get directions?"

"Fine. See you in a few days." Sara hung up the phone and wondered why she felt as if she had just given Nancy Thomas exactly what she wanted.

Harrison was packed and ready, but he regretted agreeing to accompany Greg and Nancy to Hilton Head. In the first place, he would much rather use the time to be with Sara, but when he had hinted they might be seeing each other sooner than she thought, she had been silent . . . a silence he had taken to mean that she stood by her idea that anything beyond being good friends was impossible for them.

He was depressed and withdrawn on the ride to the airport, and the news that they would have to change planes in Charlotte—a mere two hours from Sara—left him agitated and cranky. He was glad Nancy had booked them first class. It meant he was sitting across the aisle from them, which gave him some space. Once they were at cruising altitude, he reclined his chair and pretended to doze.

As usual, his thoughts drifted to Sara. Just when he thought he was getting over her, just when he thought Sara might have been right to insist on some distance, some caution, he would get a crayon drawing from Liza or a test paper with a high mark from Jefferson. These he pinned to the bulletin board above his desk. At first they went one on top of the other because he didn't know what to do with them and they seemed too precious to throw away. Later he began to spread them out so that each could be seen individually.

In the final analysis, they had all gotten to him—even Ling and Amy and the townspeople. He missed them all. But he more than missed Sara—with Sara it was more than simple thinking about her from time to time—he yearned for her. He yearned for the sound of her laughter, for the sight of her at her loom, for the sharing of ideas and conversation, for the wonder of her body next to his.

He tried to tell himself that if they had made love sooner or more often he would find it easier to get over her. But he doubted that was true. He had known some women who were very good in bed and when that had ended he hadn't had any such feelings of longing or need. Hell, a lot of the time he didn't even think about sex with Sara— he just missed having her nearby. Sometimes, especially when he sat at the counter in his kitchen and ate cold cereal while he read the morning paper, he thought about the meals she had prepared and how they had gone beyond simple food—they had always included conversation and camaraderie and even occasional surprises.

New York had definitely lost some of its hold, since his return from North Carolina. His apartment had begun to seem particularly deserted and without personality. It was a decorator's idea of what the upwardly mobile west side couple should have. Catherine had had the place done, and he had never changed it since her death.

No, Sara Peters had been wrong to think distance would temper his need for her. If anything, it had embellished his image of her to the point where he was beginning to suspect he might actually be in . . .

"Sir?"

The stewardess stood over him, smiling vivaciously, flirting with her eyes. "Would you like something to eat? Or just a pillow?"

Harrison studied her for a moment. She was prettier

than Sara in the conventional sense. He did that a lot lately—compared other women to Sara. "Food sounds good," he answered.

Surely it wouldn't hurt to call Sara from the airport. He could see how she reacted to the idea of his being so nearby. Hell, if he got the right vibes from her, he could ditch Hilton Head, rent a car right then and there, and be at the farm in time to greet the kids as they came home from school. Nancy and Greg would understand. In fact, they'd probably be thrilled.

For the rest of the flight to Charlotte he ate the meal, talked across the aisle to Greg and Nancy, flipped through the airline magazine, and turned down three more attempts by the stewardess to assist him with any problem.

"What time is our flight to Hilton Head?" he asked as the three of them walked into the terminal.

"Around two, I think." Nancy was being very mysterious about plans. She had insisted on holding all three tickets instead of giving Harrison his to carry.

"I need to make a call. I'll meet you at the gate." Harrison scanned the departure screen looking for the flight to Hilton Head. "Oh, there it is—Concourse C— you guys go on and I'll be right there."

"Well, actually . . ." Suddenly Nancy seemed a little nervous.

The public address system interrupted the rest of what she had been about to say. "Will Mr. and Mrs. Gregory Thomas please meet your party at the baggage claim area?"

"You're meeting friends here?" Harrison was confused. He had no idea they even knew anyone in Charlotte. They certainly had never mentioned it.

"You'd better tell him," Greg urged as Nancy led the way to the escalator to the baggage claim area.

"Well, actually, Harrison, Greg and I have a wonderful surprise for you."

It was at that exact moment that Harrison saw Sara

waiting by the baggage carousel, scanning the crowd and holding a small hand-lettered sign that read *Greg and Nancy Thomas*.

At first she thought she was seeing things. Harry, looking more wonderful than she had thought possible, was walking straight toward her. So taken was she with actually seeing him, after so many hours of imagining him, that she did not notice the handsomely dressed couple with him.

"Harry," she said as she took a step toward him. But then she stopped. The expression on his face was as startled as her own. He should have been smiling with delight at having put one over on her, but instead he just stared at her, as if he too, were having trouble believing his eyes.

"You must be Sara." A small, dark-haired woman with long beautifully manicured nails and dressed in a designer warm-up suit grinned at her. "I'm Nancy, and this is Greg."

Sara gathered her senses and her manners and returned their handshakes. But her eyes kept returning to Harry.

"Uh, Nancy," he said, turning to his friend. "Don't you have a bit of explaining to do?"

The woman giggled with delight. In fact, she actually clapped her hands together as if applauding her own handiwork. "Isn't this wonderful?"

Harry and Sara simply glanced at her.

"Why don't I get the bags?" Greg said and escaped before anyone could stop him.

"Well, it just could not have worked out better." Nancy turned to Harry first. "You see, darling, when I realized we'd be changing planes in Charlotte I called Sara—you had indicated she was close by—because I thought it would be fun to meet her, have dinner together . . ."

"Our plane leaves at two," Harry reminded her. He was feeling annoyance—that Nancy had plotted behind his back, that in her plot she had gotten Sara to drive all the way here for fifteen minutes at the baggage claim, that there would be no time for him and Sara to talk privately. Sara would be unfailingly polite, and he wouldn't have a clue as to whether she wanted him to visit her or not.

"Yes. But that's tomorrow, darling, or the day after that if we like," Nancy said off-handedly. "It's the beauty of first class. You can pretty well name your own schedule, and they'll fall all over themselves to accommodate you."

"When Nancy called, I asked her if she and Greg would like to come out to the farm for supper," Sara added. She could not for the life of her understand why she was helping Nancy explain what was clearly a dreadful situation. Harry was upset . . . maybe even angry.

"And then when I called to let her know our flight times, Sara insisted on coming to meet us. You do understand that she had not an inkling we would have you with us?" Again the delighted giggle as she clapped her hands in applause of her matchmaking.

Greg chose that moment to rejoin the group with the luggage piled on a metal cart manned by a skycap. "All set?"

"I suppose you knew all about this," Harry asked quietly.

Greg looked slightly sheepish, but then he grinned. "Guilty . . . to a point. I didn't know the business about Sara coming to meet us until we were actually on the flight down here." He smiled at Sara. "Is the car nearby?"

Glad to be able to go into action Sara started leading the way toward the automatic doors. "Out front. I brought the van so we could be comfortable. As it turns out we'll definitely need the extra room." She glanced at Harry who was bringing up the rear. No, Harry was not happy about this. *Mark that down, Sara, the man does not like surprises . . . not at all.*

At the curb, Harry dismissed the skycap and took over

the loading of the luggage as Sara held the cart. Nancy and Greg tipped the skycap and then climbed into the van.

"I'm glad to see you," Sara said quietly as she held the back door open while Harry placed the bags inside. And since she was nervous, she fell back on her habit of babbling. "You know, Harry, she meant well and it's just for one night. The kids are going to be thrilled, not to mention Ling. Oh, and I'd better call Amos. . . ."

She was talking quietly but nonstop, ticking the names off on her fingertips, as he pushed in the last bag and closed the van doors.

"We probably should make a stop at the grocery store on the way," she said, daring to look directly at him for the first time since spotting him in the airport.

It had never occurred to him that he would see her again so suddenly. In his fantasies they had run happily toward each other, colliding in a passionate embrace, kissing each other madly until neither could breathe. In his fantasies, Greg and Nancy had been nowhere in sight and the setting had been far more romantic than midday at the airport. He frowned.

She noticed. "It's just for one evening. I think you can muddle through," she said tersely and turned toward the driver's side of the van.

He tapped her on the shoulder and smiled when she turned. He pulled her into his embrace, his mouth finding hers before she had a chance to protest. So it was midday, so it was an airport, so it was not exactly the stuff of Hollywood—it was Sara, and in that moment, that was all that mattered.

They finally became aware of honking horns and whistles and calls from surrounding cars. When they broke apart, Nancy and Greg had turned full around and were grinning at them from the backseat like a couple of delighted matchmakers.

"You drive," Sara said and handed him the keys.

He followed her to the passenger side and opened the

door for her, handing her into the van as an excuse to touch her again.

Then he dashed around the front of the vehicle, grinning and giving the high sign to a couple of cabbies who called out their comments on the scene they had just witnessed.

"Well, I think we're going to have a splendid visit," Nancy announced as soon as he had pulled away from the curb. "And what lovely country, Sara. Tell us all about it."

The ride went quickly. Nancy and Greg asked lots of questions and were genuinely interested in whatever she could offer in the way of history and folklore. Before they knew it, Harry was pulling into the grocery store parking lot.

"Why don't you ladies go get what you need, and I'll take Greg over to the newspaper office," Harry said. "I'd like Ed Bower to meet the other half of the team he helped win the biggest case of their careers."

Nancy drew lots of polite, curious stares in the grocery store, but because she was with Sara she was instantly accepted as okay. Sara discovered that the woman had a natural ability to relate to people, putting them at ease with her friendliness and delightful sense of humor. So, she was somewhat surprised when Nancy turned serious as they waited in the checkout line.

"I hope you aren't upset with me, Sara. I know I took a risk, not telling either of you, but . . ."

"It's all right," Sara said, tempted to pat the woman's arm in comfort.

Nancy grinned. "If you could have seen your face . . . not to mention Harrison's . . . You call him Harry, don't you? No one ever called him Harry—I like it."

Sara laughed. "He hated it at first, but then Liza . . . that's my little girl, well, not actually, she's a foster child, but . . ."

Nancy smiled. "I can't wait to meet the children."

By the time they were back in the van it was as if the

four of them had been friends for years. The conversation was easy and lively as Harry maneuvered the van along the curving road out to the farm.

Sara pointed out landmarks, including the place where they had found Harry lying on the side of the road.

"There's no historical marker yet?" Harry actually sounded disappointed.

"The historical committee meets next month. I'm sure it's on the agenda. You know how we Southerners love to put up commemorative plaques . . . especially about Yankee casualties."

The first sound they heard when they pulled up to the house was an earsplitting shriek. "Har-r-r-y!"

Liza came bounding off the porch and into his arms almost before he had a chance to get out of the van. "Harry, you came, too?" The wonder of it was almost too much for Liza, but not so much that she didn't peer over his shoulder to study the beautifully dressed lady and the handsome man getting out of the backseat. "Are those your friends?" she asked.

"Yep. That's Nancy and Greg Thomas."

"Mr. and Mrs. Thomas to you, young lady," Sara warned.

Liza wriggled away from Harry and approached the strangers. "Hi, I'm Liza. Will you read me a story sometime?"

"She's very shy," Sara noted dryly.

"Yeah," Harry added. "I'd be careful on the story thing—it's a rite of initiation."

"Did you pass?" Nancy asked Harry with a laugh.

"I think so."

"Hi, Harry."

L. C. had joined the noisy group and stood slightly apart. Harry walked over to him and offered him a handshake. "How's it going, sport?"

"Not too bad. You here to stay?" He regarded Harry with a scowl and more than a touch of sarcasm.

Sara rolled her eyes. "L. C.," she said warningly. "He's missed you," she added for Harry's benefit.

"I'm here to check up on you. How's the ball handling coming? The Knickerbockers need a point guard next season."

L. C. would not be so easily cajoled. "It's okay," he muttered, stubbing the toe of his shoe in the dirt and not looking at Harry.

Harry seemed at a loss for what to do next. He was clearly taken aback at L. C.'s attitude toward him.

"Maybe we could have a game later," Harry said.

L. C. simply shrugged.

Nancy and Greg had gone uncustomarily quiet as they observed the family drama taking place before them. Sara knew Harry was disappointed, but there was little she could do about that.

"Well, come on in," she invited and led the way to the house. "On the chance you might agree to stay the night I made up the guest room." She glanced at Harry and added, "Jefferson's room."

"Is my room still there?" Harry asked Liza.

"Mama made the bed back into a couch, but we could pull it out again, couldn't we, Mama?"

"That's the beauty of a sofa bed," Sara observed with a smile.

Supper was a lively affair with Ling and Amy joining them and Amos and his wife, Lucy, dropping by for dessert. There was a great deal of laughter as everyone related their version of the rescue-of-Harry story, and they stayed at the table for a long time.

"Don't you just love it when it stays light so late?" Nancy asked later as she and Sara were clearing the dishes.

"It's my favorite time of year," Sara agreed. She was standing at the sink washing the dishes that the dishwasher had been unable to hold and watching Harry, Greg, Ling, and Amy play basketball. Even L. C. had gotten into the game and seemed for the moment to have forgotten he was supposed to be cool toward Harry. Amos acted as referee while Liza and Lucy stood on the sidelines playing cheerleader.

"You're good for him," Nancy observed quietly, standing next to Sara and watching the game as she wiped the dishes.

"Well . . ."

"Now don't duck me on this. This is going to take some work . . . that is, if you want it to happen?"

Sara blinked. "Excuse me?"

Nancy placed one hand on her hip and sighed as if she were dealing with a not-so-bright child. "Well, Harrison . . . Harry . . . is in love with you if I'm any judge of these things at all, and trust me, I am a master at sizing such things up. So, we have to make plans if you want it all to work out."

And Sara had thought of herself as direct. She focused on the dishes for a minute, then asked, "Did you know Catherine?"

"Catherine? Of course, I knew her. We weren't exactly bosom buddies, but I knew her. We spent time together."

"What was she like?"

"Spoiled, rich, selfish."

Sara frowned. "But she loved Harry." It was a statement waiting for affirmation.

Again, Nancy sighed, but this time it was a sigh of frustration. "Yes. Catherine loved Harry . . . as much as she was capable of loving someone other than herself."

Sara smiled. "I take it I'm not exactly getting an unbiased opinion here."

"I didn't care for her—it's true. She wasn't right for Harry. He deserved someone . . . better."

"Did he love her?" This one she knew the answer to. She knew it every time she recalled that first night when he had kissed her while calling for Catherine.

Nancy paused. "At first, yeah. He was really head over

heels. I remember when he first brought her over to the house. He couldn't take his eyes off her. She was incredibly beautiful and she knew how to make the most of that. Plus her . . . drama, I guess you'd call it, fascinated him. She was so passionate about her acting that I think Harry assumed that that passion would transfer to him.''

''And then?''

''He was so good to her, buying her anything she wanted, even when he couldn't really afford it. She came from money. So does he for that matter, but there's money and then there's m-o-n-e-y. She would have these whims—a house in the country, a vacation in Paris, complete, of course, with shopping at all the designer houses. And when she began to face the fact that she would never be more than a bit player, she began to take it out on Harry.''

Sara was watching the game in the yard as she listened. She could not suppress a smile when she saw Harry raise L. C. up for a slam dunk over Greg's attempts to guard him. ''Harry told me she didn't want children.''

Nancy gave a mirthless laugh. ''Harry adores kids— look at him.'' She indicated the game. ''Heavens, when my kids were babies they thought of Harry as a favorite uncle. They still do for that matter. But Catherine . . .''

''Well, maybe . . . I mean, if she was pursuing a career . . . that's understandable.''

Nancy stopped drying the meat platter and stared at her. ''My God, you can't be that charitable. The woman led him on, promising *someday*. Well, someday never came.''

''You mean because she died.''

''I mean because she killed herself rather than face the fact that she would never be Meryl Streep.''

Sara was stunned. Harry had given no indication. She had viewed his marriage as perfectly unblemished, a model of happiness marred by unspeakable tragedy.

''Harry didn't tell you?''

Sara just shook her head.

"I'm not surprised. For a long time he blamed himself—if only this, if only that. Then it was as if he just decided to shut that part of his life away. . . ."

"He told me they had been planning a trip when she died."

"Harry thought if they got away—just the two of them—they could rebuild what he thought they had in the beginning. Harry does not give up easily. It was hard for him to admit he had made a mistake."

"But the trip never happened?"

"No. Catherine knew how to play the moment for all the drama she could wring out of it. She left him a note that said something like *Forgive me, darling, but I left on my trip a day early.*"

"That's awful." Suddenly Sara was angry. She'd never met Catherine and she was always reluctant to think ill of the dead, but this was terribly self-centered. "How devastating that must have been . . . how . . . oh, that makes me so angry. How could she do that to anyone, much less Harry? He's so wonderful and caring and . . ." She was talking to herself now.

"As I was saying, I think we have to get busy, my dear," Nancy said with a grin. "Being alone has gotten to be something of a habit with Harry. I hardly have to tell you about that. You've got that habit down pretty good from what I can tell. Add to that the fact that Harry's been gun-shy ever since."

The comment about Sara's life had jarred her back to reality. "It won't work, Nancy. I appreciate what you're trying to do—I know all the signs are there—but it's not going to work. You can't run a serious relationship when one person's life is New York and the other's is Tate's Mill."

"Let me ask you one simple question. Do you love him?"

Sara laughed. "That's hardly a simple question."

"Come on, gut feeling, yes or no?"

The game had ended. The others were thronging toward the back door. Nancy stood her ground. "Well?"

"Yes, but . . ."

Nancy held up her hand to forestall anything more Sara might add. "No buts allowed." Then she turned the full radiance of her considerable charm on the others. "So, who won?"

TWELVE

The rest of the evening passed in a feast of food, laughter, storytelling, and good friendship. Sara began to feel as if she had known Nancy forever and gradually began to appreciate Greg's dry sense of humor. For Liza and L.C. it was like discovering a favorite aunt and uncle.

The kids were spellbound as Nancy showed them pictures of her own children. "This is our daughter, Elise. She's twelve. And here's Jason. He's ten."

"I'm six—almost seven," Liza announced. "And L.C. is ten."

"Well, my goodness I'll bet you'd be just great friends with our kids then," Nancy said.

"When can we meet them?" Liza, as usual, saw no obstacle to setting a plan into action.

"Well, let's see. They're staying with their grandmother in New York right now. Do you know where New York is?"

"Of course," Liza piped up before L. C. could form an answer. "It's up there where Harry lives."

"That's right. And just like we came down here to visit you, maybe one day you'll come to New York and see us."

Both children's eyes grew round with wonder at the prospect. "Could we fly?" L. C. asked almost breathless with anticipation.

"I don't see why not," Greg said. Then he frowned. "Of course, you may want to take an airplane the first time. It's a pretty long trip. Your arms might get awfully tired."

L. C. just stared at him at first; then he started to giggle. "Take an airplane . . . that's good . . . you're funny."

"Liza, L. C., it's way past bedtime," Sara said gently.

"I've heard that you two like stories," Nancy said. "How about if Greg and I help you get ready for bed and then read you a story?"

The kids were all for that idea and raced off to choose their favorite book.

"Nancy, you don't have to do this," Sara began.

"Now, no arguments. I'm missing my own little devils, so humor me." She started toward the stairs and then turned to Harry. "Why don't you and Sara take a walk?" she said nonchalantly.

When Greg and Nancy had disappeared into the children's rooms, Harry turned to Sara and smiled. "Subtle, isn't she?"

"I like her," Sara replied. "Greg, too. They're wonderful with the kids."

Harry nodded. "So, how 'bout that walk?"

It was awkward at first. They hadn't really been alone yet. They walked for several steps in silence.

"I've been thinking," Harry said as they strolled along. "What if Nancy and Greg go on to Hilton Head and I stay here?" He focused on dissecting a leaf he had pulled off of a low hanging branch, carefully separating it from its stem. "Maybe we could drive down to South Carolina Saturday. Sunday is Mother's Day, you know. I'd like to see Jefferson."

"I'm sure he'd like to see you, too." Sara knew it was not an answer, but the thoughts she was having were so jumbled. On the one hand her heart had leapt at the very idea of having him back in her life if only for a few days. On the other hand, what was the point? The first time they had had to say goodbye had been so hard on the kids . . . and her. In some ways they had just started to get over that.

"Is that a yes? As in 'Yes, Harry, we'd be thrilled to have you stay the week?' "

"I . . . guess so."

"Not exactly the ringing endorsement I had hoped for, but I'll take what I can get." He looked down at her and smiled, then walked on.

"Actually I had thought of taking the kids out of school a couple of days and making a little vacation out of it. With the art fair season at hand, it won't be easy to get away once school is out."

"Sounds like a good idea."

"And Charleston has a lot of historical significance."

"That's true."

"Ling can take care of things here."

"You've certainly thought this all out." He waited, and when she didn't add anything new, said "So, do I get to come along or not?"

"Well, sure. I just thought you ought to know what was involved."

"Well, let's see now. I get to be with you and the kids in one of the most romantic cities in the country in spring. I get to see Jefferson. I get to be with you. I get my vacation, which is why I left work in the first place. I get to be with you. . . ." This last he said softly and stopped walking as he pulled her into his arms. "Sounds good to me," he whispered just before he kissed her.

Reliving his touch, his kiss, the feel of his body next to hers had been a frequent daydream of Sara's over the past several weeks. Now that he was actually holding her, she realized her imagination had failed her.

"I've missed you, Sara," he whispered just before

deepening the kiss. "Actually," he said, "I've been thinking quite a lot about that old willow bed . . . how comfortable it was . . . how much nicer it would be if you shared
it with me."

In truth she had entertained the same fantasies, but there
the resemblance apparently ended. For in her dreams his
intentions went beyond sex. They included impassioned
statements of his longing for her while they had been
apart. They included declarations of undying love. They
included—in their most fully developed stage—plans for
a life together . . . a marriage.

In reality, he had asked for nothing more than to come
to her bed. She pulled away. Sanity prevailed. Harry was
back, but for how long? A day? A week? No, it had hurt
too much when he had left before . . . even though she
had warned herself to have no regrets. She wouldn't do
that to herself again. "We'd better get back," she said.

Now it was his turn to be confused. "Didn't you hear
what I said?" He was close to shaking her, but he re-
strained himself.

"You said you want us to go to bed . . . specifically
to my bed."

Why did she have to make it sound so . . . callous? "I
didn't mean it that way," he said. "Will you please look
at me?" She had been studying her feet since running out
of things to do to her person to show that she was finished
with any romantic notions he might have.

Her head snapped up, and her expression in the moonlight was pleasant and completely impersonal.

This time he did take her by the shoulders, though he
stopped short of actually shaking her. "Don't you get it?
I love you," he growled.

She smiled and pulled free. "Forgot to add that little
detail before, did you? Well, get this straight, Harry
Hixon, I may just be a plain country girl, but I know bull
when I hear it. We have something very nice as friend-
ships go. If you insist on adding sex to that every time

we get together you're going to mess that up royally. You can't want your itch scratched and try to cover it over with what you think I want to hear. You got that?'' She didn't wait for his answer but started back toward the house.

After several steps, she realized he wasn't coming after her and could not resist the urge to see what he was doing, so she turned around.

He was standing where she had left him staring at her. ''I'm still going to Charleston,'' he called to her, then he turned and took off at a loping pace as he jogged into the woods and disappeared from view.

Back at the house, she ignored the curious looks from Greg and Nancy who were sitting at the kitchen table. ''How about some more of that lemon pie?'' she said, busying herself with plates, forks, cutting the pie, anything to keep her back to them for a few minutes.

''Where's Harri . . . Harry,'' Greg asked.

Sara shrugged as she set the dishes before them. ''He decided he wanted to go for a run. He used to do that sometimes . . . when his knee was healing. He knows the paths pretty well. He'll be fine. How about some milk?''

The three of them ate pie and made strained small talk.

''We really ought to get some sleep,'' Nancy noted finally. ''Sara, if you'll excuse us?''

Sara had been lost in thought. In fact, for the last several minutes there had been no conversation at the table, only long questioning looks between Greg and Nancy and Sara's jumping at the slightest sound that came from the yard.

''Of course. I'm sorry. Let me come up and show you where everything is.'' She led the way to what had been Jefferson's room and now served as the guest room. She pointed out where towels and supplies were kept in the bathroom and then left the two of them, promising them a hearty country breakfast in the morning. They said their goodnights, and Sara escaped back down the stairs.

She cleaned up the dishes from the pie and milk, all the while keeping an ear open for Harry's return. She leafed through a magazine and waited. She wandered through the living room straightening pillows. She made up the sofabed in the sunroom for Harrison. And still he was not back.

She walked out onto the porch and searched the darkness for a sight of him, for the sound of him, but heard nothing but the crickets and the wind in the pines. So, with a sigh she went back inside, turned out all the lights but one and went upstairs.

She had only been in bed a few minutes when she heard the squeak of the back screen door, then the soft thud of his footsteps through the kitchen and into the sunroom. After a few minutes she heard the sound of the downstairs shower running and then the click of the light she had left on for him. Then there was silence.

She lay awake for a long time. Just before she went to sleep she looked over at the undisturbed empty side of the large double bed. Ever since Harry had gone back to New York, Sara had taken to sleeping on one side of the bed. She had given in to the fantasy of his being there—permanently there. On more than one night, she had pretended that they would someday share that bed as man and wife. Before she'd known him she'd always slept in the middle. But even though they had never shared the bed, she had saved that space for him since their night of love by the creek. She had imagined them there together, married, raising the children, growing old. She looked at the space now, thought of him downstairs, thought of his proposition tonight, and moved determinedly toward the center of the bed.

Harry hadn't remembered the sofabed being quite so lumpy. He flopped onto his stomach and pummeled the flat pillow, trying to pump some life into it. Then he flopped back onto his back and stared out at the silhouette of the pines against the sky.

He'd been as surprised as she when he said it. I love you. Hell, he hadn't even known he was about to say it. But it hadn't been a damn line like she thought. It hadn't been a ploy to get her in the sack. Nothing so simple as that—that would have been easy.

But no. He had to go and say he loved her and mean it. And worse yet she hadn't believed him—wouldn't believe him now. Talk about poor timing. No wonder she'd been ticked off. She had this thing about him thinking she was unsophisticated . . . always had. Now she thought he'd tried a big city move on her to get her to go to bed with him. Hell, she would have gone to bed with him right there under the stars; she had been as ready as he was.

But no, he had to try for something better, something more . . . permanent, more binding. Making love in the house . . . in her room . . . in that bed he'd imagined her in every night since going back to New York—in his mind that had meant a step toward a real commitment.

Part of that had been what he was trying to communicate while they walked and he'd asked about staying the week. What the hell did she think that had been about? After all, with two kids along they weren't exactly going off on some cruise of mad passion. They'd be lucky to enjoy a kiss now and then along the way. Didn't that prove that he was in this for more than just sex? What did a guy have to do to get to this woman?

He turned over and buried his face in the pillow, then turned back again. The trees were still there, forming a sort of skyline against the brightness of the moonlight.

Of course, she didn't think this could work—him in New York, her here. That could be part of it. Blurting out his love for her was not exactly a way to calm those particular misgivings. But again, it wasn't as though he'd intended to say the words. Not that he hadn't thought about saying them . . . actually, what he'd thought about was her saying them, usually in the heat of their lovemaking, something he had imagined a number of times in graphic detail over the past several weeks.

He heard the squeak of a bed overhead, and his ears perked up. But then he heard Greg's cough and relaxed. He might actually have to murder Nancy. After all, things in New York had been going along okay. So, he didn't have Sara in New York. So, he was lonely and miserable and the thought of spending any time with another woman was unbelievably annoying. So, his life had deteriorated pretty much to going to work, grabbing some take-out, and falling asleep in front of the tube. At least he was able to sleep—unlike tonight.

He tossed around a bit more, then sat on the side of the bed. He might as well get up. He wandered into the kitchen and rummaged around for something to eat. Spotting the pie he got a fork and started eating right from the dish.

The woman was a hell of a cook. Catherine had never cooked. He wasn't sure whether she had known how or not—she just never did. He used to tease her about turning the stove into a planter, a joke she had failed to see the humor in.

He ate the pie in layers—the meringue, then the filling, then the crust. Sara ate it that way, too, he remembered. They had laughed about it.

Sara had a good sense of humor. She also had one hell of a temper. He smiled remembering some of the encounters they'd had early on.

He finished the pie and then opened the refrigerator. Taking out the milk, he drank directly from the carton and then remembered how Sara had gotten mad at Jefferson for doing that exact same thing one day after a basketball game.

She was good with the kids—really good. A real mother. Catherine had been too selfish to be a good mother

. . . even if they had had kids. Of course, that had never been a possibility. He felt the now familiar nugget of fury at what Catherine had done. She had seemed to share his dream of a family life, promising someday when her career was launched, reminding him the memory of the critics was only as long as your most recent role, agreeing to go on the trip . . . mark the start of their life as a family. . . .

He stood there with the refrigerator door open and the empty milk carton in his hand as he recalled finding her that morning, reading the note, realizing how little that planned life together had meant to her . . . how little he'd meant to her. He had thought he loved Catherine, but over time he had come to understand that he had only wanted to love her. She had never allowed him to do that.

He closed the refrigerator and set the empty milk carton in the sink. He wandered into the living room, plopping onto the couch, picking up a book report L. C. had brought to show Greg and Nancy earlier. The boy had not shown much interest in sharing his work with him. With the exception of the basketball game the kid had definitely kept his distance. Harry wondered what that was all about. Why was he being singled out? L. C. had been really friendly with Greg and Nancy. Harry realized that L. C.'s attitude toward him hurt—that it mattered a lot to him.

He sat there for a long time thinking about how it might be to have a son like L. C., a daughter like Liza. He thought about being married to Sara, having a kid of their own . . . a boy, no, a girl who looked just like her . . . twins, maybe.

He thought about his parents and the home they had made for their children—a bit unconventional perhaps, given all the traveling and the money—there had always been laughter, fun, pride, and love. He'd always wanted that for himself . . . always assumed it would come with growing up, like going to college, passing the bar, setting up his practice, getting married. . . .

*   *   *

Sara found Harry on the couch sound asleep when she came down to start breakfast and help Ling with the chores. He was wearing shorts and a t-shirt and on his chest was the report L. C. had proudly shown everyone but Harry the night before.

She stood there watching him, enjoying the hand-someness of his face relaxed in sleep. The mornings could still be cool in the mountains so she got one of her afghans and covered him. Standing there looking at him she couldn't resist the instinct to smooth his hair away from his brow, to caress the stubble of beard that had developed in the night. But when he stirred, she turned quickly and escaped to the kitchen before he could wake and find her watching him.

The house did not stay quiet for long. By the time she had done the chores, the children were up. There's a certain amount of commotion that comes with the territory of children getting off to school in the morning. And no matter how hard they tried to be quiet, they could not contain their normal exuberance. So, by the time they left, Greg and Nancy had wandered into the kitchen and Harry had appeared, unshaven but dressed in jeans.

"You look like hell," Nancy observed as she poured coffee for Harry while Sara stood on the back porch waving to the children.

"Good morning to you, too," Harry growled.

"Sleep well?" Sara asked as she came back into the house.

Nancy and Greg beamed and nodded; Harry just stared at her.

"Good. How about some breakfast?"

When Greg and Nancy had put the children to bed the night before, L. C. and Liza had been full of plans for going to Charleston to visit Jefferson and his family. And later Sara had mentioned that Harrison might go, too. Of course, given the silent sparks that flew whenever Sara or Harry said a word at breakfast, Nancy had her doubts the trip would actually come off.

"You are going to Charleston?" she prodded, looking first at Harry and then at Sara.

Sara made a show of stirring her coffee.

Harry muttered, "I'm going," through a mouthful of granola.

Nancy smiled and buttered her third muffin. "Well, splendid, then the two of you won't mind a bit if Greg and I head for the airport after breakfast."

Harry growled his approval, and Sara made a show of politeness. "So soon? I had thought we might at least have the day together."

"The golf course calls," Greg announced with a smile. "But we'll get together again real soon." He squeezed Sara's hand.

The silence lengthened as Sara and Harry avoided eye contact.

"Sara, these are the most sinfully delicious things." Nancy made a show of taking a bite of her muffin. "If I were any kind of cook, I'd ask for the recipe. I'm afraid my talents in the kitchen are limited to opening the freezer and popping something from a box into the microwave."

Greg laughed. "And I'd say that's putting it kindly." He dodged a mock punch from his wife and glanced at Sara.

The couple could not miss the fact that table talk was their exclusive property. Sara and Harry were very silent.

"So," Nancy said on a long sigh after another several moments of silence. "I know. Why don't the four of us drive to the airport, have lunch along the way. . . ." She glanced around for reaction. Sara seemed slightly enthusiastic. Harry was not saying no, so she continued, "Then, on your way home, the two of you could stop for a nice romantic dinner . . . just the two of you. Wouldn't that be nice?"

Sara risked a look at Harry, but he did not meet her eyes. She got up and started to clear the table. "I'd really like to come, Nancy, because it seems as if you just got here and now you're leaving already. But I have all this work that needs finishing before we leave for Charleston tomorrow, not to mention getting clothes ready for the kids . . . finding their swimming suits in case the motel has a pool. . . ."

Nancy brought her own plate and Greg's to the sink and rinsed them. "It's okay," she said with a meaningful look at Harry's back. "I understand."

"I'll take you to the airport," Harry said to Greg. Then he turned to Sara for the first time all morning. "Is that all right? I mean, can I use the van?"

"Sure. Good idea."

Nancy and Greg went to pack and say their good-byes. Harry mumbled something about Ling and escaped through the back door.

Sara sighed and set about washing the dishes, by hand.

While Greg and Harry loaded the van, Nancy stayed in the kitchen. "You know, Sara, I've known Harry for a long time. I don't know what happened last night, but it seems as if the two of you have a lot to work out. I just thought you might like to know that Greg and I think it's worth it . . . for Harry and for you."

Sara smiled and held out her arms to give Nancy a hug. "I miss you already," she said, and it was true. It had been a long time since she had met someone her own age she had taken such an instant liking to.

"We'll be seeing a lot of each other . . . I don't doubt that. You know, one of these days—however this thing with Harry comes out—you will come to New York. If nothing else, your work will bring you there. I mean, darling, you are good! Would you mind if I contacted a couple of gallery owners on your behalf?"

"Nancy, you don't have to do that."

Nancy grinned and picked up her cosmetic case. "You

Southerners and your false modesty. Believe me, Sara, this isn't some idle gesture. I'd like to see your work in New York. So, if you think you're up to it . . .''

Now it was Sara's turn to laugh. "And you New Yorkers think the rest of the world is just dying to lay some claim to your city."

"Hey, like the song says . . . 'if you can make it there'. . . . So? Are you game?''

"Why not? Give it your best shot."

They walked out to the van arm in arm as Harry considered them from his position in the driver's seat. He was still frowning at her. It was going to be some trip to Charleston, Sara thought with a frown of her own.

But then Greg gave her a quick hug and whispered, "Don't let the bear get to you. He's really harmless and actually not a bad fellow."

She smiled and waved as they left, thinking that even if things never worked out with Harry, she had just made two very nice new friends.

She found herself humming the New York song as she settled in at her loom with a cup of coffee and her earphones and went to work. She figured she had several hours to work and willed herself to put everything out of her mind and concentrate on the project before her.

And for most of the morning she was successful. But then Harry came in. At first she wasn't aware of his return. She'd heard no car on the gravel drive, no squeak of the back screened door. She was working and humming along to the music on her earphones when she realized he was there watching her quietly from the doorway to the kitchen.

"When did you get back?" she asked without turning, without breaking the rhythm of her weaving. She did remove the headphones.

"We need to talk. I thought, with everybody gone, this might be a good time." He moved further into the room and sat down near the loom. "You can keep working if you like."

At first she did just that. It was an excuse for not meeting his eyes, for not looking directly at him, for not dealing with how very attracted she was to him.

"What did you want to talk about?" She pulled hard on the beater, released it, and sent the shuttle flying through the next shed.

"Why don't we start with last night?"

"Okay."

"I'm sorry for the mixed signals and for upsetting you and for maybe assuming too much." She opened her mouth to say something, but he stopped her. "But I'm not at all sorry for what I said."

"About wanting to go to bed."

He gave an exasperated sigh and leaned toward her, his eyes so focused on her that she could feel the insistence of them. "About loving you," he said.

She allowed several passes of the shuttle before she paused and turned to look at him directly for the first time since he had sat down.

"I don't want you to love me," she said quietly. "It makes everything too complicated." *Liar!* a voice from deep inside her shouted.

"But you were willing to *make* love with me . . . out there under the trees. You're not going to get away with denying that one."

"I . . . no, that's true. For a moment there—"

"Just for a moment?"

Now it was her turn to heave an exasperated sigh. "Look, when you showed up at the airport yesterday it was . . . it took me back. I wasn't ready for that. What we had shared that night when you left was still too fresh. And so . . . last night . . . well, I . . . for a minute I . . ."

During her weak attempts at explanation he had gotten up and begun to pace. He was behind her and in some ways that made things easier, so she did not turn around. But then he stood behind her, pulling her against him, touching her shoulders and neck and face.

"Did you want me, Sara? That's what you're accusing me of . . . wanting you . . . and I did. I want you now." His voice was low and caressing in tandem with his hands on her. After a moment, he felt her begin to relax under the hypnotic influence of his words and the massage. "I've thought about that night we spent together every day since I left. I've dreamed about it, about you, about how it would be. And you thought about that night, too, didn't you, Sara?"

Without letting go of her he sat so that he was opposite her on the bench. Her eyes were closed, and she simply nodded in answer to his question.

"I love you, Sara. When I said it last night I was as surprised as you were, but here in the hard light of day, I know it's true. I love you."

He kissed her then, tenderly, gently, allowing her time to pull away. And when she didn't, he turned her so that she half lay across his lap, and he kissed her more ardently.

"Ah, Harry." It was a sigh of surrender and something like resignation, but her arms came around him and she kissed him back.

They stayed that way for several minutes—kissing and touching without saying anything more. Harry could not get past the incredible bittersweetness the moment seemed to hold. It was as if they were saying goodbye again.

"Talk to me," he said finally as he helped her to sit up and led her to the more comfortable sofa. "Tell me what you're thinking, Sara." He was painfully aware of the fact that there had been no matching declaration of love from her lips.

"Last night," she began. "I was very . . . torn. What we had shared when you were here—all of it, not just that night by the creek—had been very . . . special. It's a time I cherish, that I'll always cherish."

"But?" He was sitting beside her now holding her hand, listening intently.

"But we are very different people, Harry. We come from very different lifestyles. And we have commitments that are already in place. We aren't like Ling and Amy—two kids just starting out, free to pick up and do as they please."

Harry grinned. "Thank God. I'm not sure I want to return to those days."

Sara frowned. "I'm serious."

He patted her hand. "I know."

"I mean you have your work—important work—and a partnership with Greg. And I have my work and the farm. And there are the children."

"I know all that."

"Don't you understand, Harry? We can't be in love. It's too hard. It's too complicated. Dammit, it hurts too much."

He had never seen her look so completely miserable. On the other hand, he felt a slight flutter of hope at her words. She'd actually come pretty close to saying she loved him.

"Come here." He cradled her against his chest and stroked her hair. "Look, we have some things to work out—there's no arguing with that—but we don't have to work them out all in one morning. What do you say we go to Charleston with the kids, see Jefferson, see the sights, and see how that goes?"

"Well . . ."

"No pressure. It would be nice to have a kiss now and then, but I seriously doubt the opportunity for anything more involved will ever present itself. You're perfectly safe. What do you say?"

"I know Jefferson would love to see you."

He laughed and hugged her hard, giving her head a playful drubbing with his knuckles. "Gee, that's really the way to make a guy feel wanted. Now get over there and get back to work while I make us some lunch."

THIRTEEN

Odessa Preston was waiting for them on her front porch. "Come in here out of the hot sun," she called as soon as they parked the van in the driveway.

The house was modest and immaculate with white aluminum siding and green shutters and a yard filled with flowers and azalea bushes.

"D.J.?" Odessa called out to someone inside the house. "Come out here and meet Sara." She wiped her hands on her apron and came down the steps to meet them. "Give me a hug, honey. It's been a month of Sundays."

She hugged Sara and each of the children and then turned to Harry. "And you . . . coming all the way from New York City just to see me? I'm honored." She grinned and hugged Harry.

"Happy Mother's Day," the children shouted, dancing around and offering her the box of candy they had watched over carefully during the entire trip.

The front screened door opened and Sara glanced up. "Jefferson," she said with a huge grin and held out her arms.

He was taller and more solidly built than she remembered, and his voice was a croak caught somewhere between child and adult. "Happy Mom's Day," he whispered as he hugged her. He turned then to Harry and gave him the ritual handshake Sara had seen him share that morning on the back porch.

Behind him came Maella. She, too, was beaming.

"Maella. I'd hardly have recognized you," Sara said. "You look wonderful."

It was true. The younger woman was markedly changed. She had put on weight, and her eyes were clear and direct. "Amazing what getting off that garbage can do for a person," she said and laughed. "I got me a job, and I'm working with kids at Jefferson's school one afternoon a week."

Yes, Sara thought, this was a new woman—more sure of herself, healthy, and unafraid.

"Meet my husband," Odessa said pulling Harry and Sara toward the porch. "D. J., Sara and her . . . friend, Harry."

D. J. was a handsome man, as reserved as Odessa was gregarious. He smiled and offered each of them his hand in welcome.

Liza, as usual, was completely at home in the new surroundings. L. C. had been very quiet on the trip down, directing his limited conversation to either Sara or Liza and ignoring Harry for the most part. And at the Preston house he stayed in the background, watching the interaction of the others and perked up only when Jefferson asked if he'd like to come with him to the schoolyard and shoot baskets with some friends.

"Me, too," Liza shouted.

"No, darling," Odessa said catching the girl before she could run after the boys. "Let's you and me go out to the kitchen and make up a batch of chocolate chip cookies." Then she turned to Harry. "You know, there's lots to see down in the historic section of town—stuff these children would be fidgeting through if you try to take them along.

Why don't you and Sara go on and spend the afternoon looking around?''

Harry grinned at her. "That's a very good idea, Odessa. That is, if you're sure there's nothing we can help you with here.''

"Not a thing. Now get going." And she punctuated her order with a broad wink.

"Thanks, Odessa," Harry said and went in search of Sara.

They parked down by the Battery, where the battle of Fort Sumter had been both visible and audible, and decided a carriage was the best way to see the sights. Their driver was an older man whose grandfather had been a slave. He knew his city and its stories like he knew his own family history. For more than an hour he regaled them with tales of the charms and scandals that were Charleston.

The rest of the afternoon they walked through the old section, looking in shop windows, stopping now and then to marvel at the size of the azaleas and their fragrance, and picking up brochures of tours they might want to take with the children the following day.

"We'd better get back," Sara said as they stood outside one of the many intricately designed iron fences and considered the gardens beyond.

"One minute more," Harry said, and taking her hand he led the way down the street.

"Where are we going?"

He seemed to be searching for something and finally found it. A garden gate stood open near one of the historic houses. "Come here," he said and led the way toward an arbor of grape vines that sheltered a small wrought iron settee and a fountain.

"Harry, I don't think we're supposed to be here.''

"Good. That heightens the thrill of it.''

"Of what?''

He kissed her then and continued kissing her for several

moments. Then he just stood there holding her, and the only sounds were the birds in the willow and the soft tinkle of the water from the fountain.

"Okay," he said after a long moment. "We can safely return to Odessa's now."

"What does that mean?"

"It means that Odessa would never forgive me if I took this whole afternoon and did not kiss you once."

"You expect her to check?" Sara was laughing as they exited the garden and headed back to the car.

"I expect her to take one look at us and *know*."

And he was right. Odessa studied both their faces closely the minute they walked into the kitchen, and then she smiled. "Supper, everybody," she called happily. "The lovers have returned."

"I'm sorry ma'am, but I have only one room reserved in that name."

Sara had insisted on going into the motel office to register while Harry waited with the children. "This is our trip," she had told him. "You can pay for your room if you like, but I am handling the rest of it."

"Well, we need another room," she told the desk clerk now.

The manager smiled patiently. "Ma'am, this is the height of the azalea season. Even out here on Isle of Palm, there are no other rooms."

They had no choice. She gave the man her credit card and accepted the key he offered.

"Problem?" Harry asked when she returned to the van.

"They only had one room. I know I asked Odessa to reserve two. . . ." Sara puzzled over the situation for a minute and then looked at Harry who was laughing.

"Odessa," he said.

And the light dawned. "I wondered why she was so anxious to handle the room reservations for me," Sara said, and then she started to grin and shake her head.

"Does this mean we got no place to stay?" L. C. demanded from the back.

"We've got a place to stay, sport," Harry assured him as he eased the van around the corner of the building to the parking place in front of their room.

At least the room had two queen-sized beds. Still Sara was frowning.

"Here's what we'll do," Harry announced as he put the bags down and surveyed the situation. "It'll be a little like camp—boys over here and girls over there. L. C., get me that piece of clothesline rope from the backseat."

In a few minutes he had rigged the rope the length of the room separating the two beds.

"Now for the wall," he said, checking the dresser drawers until he found the extra blankets.

Liza was giggling, and even L. C. was getting involved, helping Harry to hang the blankets over the rope.

"I think I saw this in a movie once," Sara observed wryly.

Harry nodded. "Clark Gable . . . Claudette Colbert."

"Who are they?" L. C. asked.

"Movie stars . . . before your time," Sara said. "Now let's get ready for bed. Odessa is expecting us all for church in the morning, and it's already very late."

Once the children were settled for the night, Harry and Sara sat on the small balcony outside their room, enjoying the warm night and the sea breeze.

"It's been a wonderful day," Harry observed.

"Doesn't Jefferson look great? And Maella! I just can't get over the change in her."

"It was the right thing Sara—letting Jefferson go with his own family. I know it hurt, but now you can see it was for the best." Harry reached across and took her hand and squeezed it.

Sara nodded. "Jefferson's one of the lucky ones. He has a family that loves him and wants him. For some of the others it's not so simple."

"Like L. C.?" Harry remembered the story of how L. C.'s family had left him at the gas station and apparently never even checked to see if he was all right.

Sara nodded. "And Tommy Lee. Although in his case it was physical abuse. Lord when that child came to me . . ." She just shook her head and did not say anything else.

"What about Liza? Surely there was other family?"

"Yeah. There was an aunt—her mother's sister. But she lives out west somewhere—Colorado, I think. She works and isn't married. Her paternal grandparents are still living, but they're divorced and apparently there had been bad blood between them and their son."

"What about adoption? I mean there must have been some interested couples—people who couldn't have children of their own."

Sara shrugged. "I told you about the one couple who took Liza for a trial period and then couldn't handle the nightmares. For L. C., well, there hasn't been anyone. Unfortunately most people want infants, and L. C. is too old. Believe it or not, so is Liza."

"Did they ever try tracing L. C.'s family?"

"Yeah, but with no luck. They just kind of disappeared and also the social services office doesn't have a lot of money for that kind of thing. For all we know they could be back in North Carolina now, but nobody's looking."

They were quiet for a moment, each lost in thoughts of the children.

"It makes me mad," Harry muttered softly.

"Yeah, me, too."

Harry stood up and put his arms around her. "All the children are lucky in one way," he said.

"What's that?"

"They have you. You've made a real difference, Sara. Every one of them has a chance because of you."

"I love them," she said as if that was all the reason anyone should need.

"But you also need to think of yourself," he said. "I mean it, Sara. When are you going to think about your life, your needs, your future?"

"I have a good life." She tried hard not to sound defensive.

"You're completely satisfied?"

"Well, who is? That's ridiculous."

His hands moved over her back and shoulders. "You mean you do want more than just working and raising stray children?"

He kissed her gently at first and then with escalating passion.

"Tell me what you want, Sara," he whispered as he rained kisses over her face and neck. "Love? Adventure? Children of your own? Tell me your dreams, Sara Peters." But he did not wait for an answer. Rather he opened his mouth to fit hers.

They stood on the balcony for some time, kissing and embracing each other, hands tunneling under fabric, mouths seeking secret places of pleasure they had discovered that night they'd made love by the creek.

"We'd better go in," Sara said finally when she felt that one more minute without having Harry completely and she would explode.

Breathless, Harry pulled back and held her loosely for a moment. Then he opened the door and led the way back into the room.

"I did make one major mistake tonight," he said with a soft chuckle.

"What was that?"

He nodded toward the beds and the makeshift blanket wall. "I should have made the camps co-ed." He gave her one last chaste kiss on the forehead and a gentle push toward the other side of the curtain.

She heard him undressing and the sigh of the mattress as he lay down.

After covering Liza, Sara undressed and got into bed.

Harry was only inches away on the other side of their "wall." For a long time she lay there listening to the sounds of the night, unable to fall asleep.

"Harry," she whispered. "You asleep?"

"No." His whisper was as wide awake as she felt.

"What are you thinking about?"

There was a pause before he answered.

"That I meant it the other night when I said I love you and that I screwed up the timing royally and that I wish there were someway to take that back and do it again—the right way."

She was quiet for a minute.

"Sara?"

"What would be the right way?"

"Oh, well, the right way would be to send you flowers in the morning with an invitation to dinner at some remote and incredibly romantic place."

Quiet again.

"So is that it?" Sara asked.

"Well, yeah, pretty much . . . except for one more thing."

"What's that?"

She heard the bed give as he shifted, and she saw the shadow of him through the curtain. He had raised up on one elbow to face her. He slowly slid the blanket along the rope until he could see her.

"What's the one thing," she repeated.

"After I said I love you? You'd say it back to me."

Her eyes were now used to the darkness and the semi-light of the room, so she could see his face. He was serious.

She swallowed, knowing what he was asking, knowing they had moved beyond the realm of fantasy. "It's a big step," she whispered.

"Especially for us," he agreed.

"There are so many . . . complications."

He nodded. "New York . . . North Carolina . . ."

"My work . . . your work . . ."

"The children . . ."

He reached over and stroked her hair. "We could try," he whispered, and after a moment he added "I love you, Sara Peters."

Sara reached across and traced the outline of his face with one finger. "I love you, too, Harry."

And then they were both smiling, lying there across from each other, holding hands.

"Goodnight, Sara," he said after a while and kissed her hand before letting it go.

"Goodnight, Harry."

And in seconds they were both asleep.

L. C. wasn't at all sure what to do. On the one hand, he had made up his mind. He didn't stay where he wasn't wanted, and he sure wasn't about to be left behind again. On the other hand, he was scared. He didn't know much about this part of the country. He hadn't really planned to be here when it happened. But he liked the fact that there was the ocean and the beach. Maybe he could stow away on a boat like he'd read about in school.

He lay still for what seemed like forever after they finally stopped whispering. He'd been able to hear only snatches, but he'd heard enough. After all, Harry had left once before. The fact that he was back wasn't anything to get excited about. From what L. C. had been able to hear, Harry had come back for one reason—to try and get Sara to leave with him.

He remembered another night, another motel not as nice as this one. He'd been lying in a bed with his half brother and sister. His mother and stepfather had been in the other bed. They'd done that thing big people do when they think kids are sleeping or they want to make a baby and now they were just lying there smoking their cigarettes and fighting . . . again.

They were always fighting. His stepfather was always yelling at somebody. His mom was only happy when she wasn't the person he was yelling at. That night he'd heard them talking . . . about not wanting to bring up another man's brat . . . about it being for the best . . . about how somebody would take him in.

Then he hadn't understood what was being said. Only the next day when they'd stopped at the gas station and sent him to the bathroom and then driven away . . . only then had it started to come together.

But now he was older and smarter. He knew what Harry was saying when he told Sara she needed to look after what she wanted. He asked about whether there had been any families interested in him. He'd also heard the silence when Sara had said there hadn't been anybody interested because he was too old. He knew what Harry Hixon had been thinking then.

And then he'd heard them kissing and talking about love and stuff. Yeah, they would leave—both of them this time. They'd probably take Liza. Harry seemed to have a thing for Liza and besides girls were easier. That's what his stepfather had said. Yeah, they'd go to New York . . . right after they turned him over to Ms. James, the social worker.

Maybe Ling and Amy would let him stay with them.

No. They'd want their own kids. Everybody wanted their own kids . . . not some reject.

The rain woke Sara. She glanced over to the other bed and saw the lump that would be L. C.—that child loved to burrow into the covers. The spot where Harry had slept was empty. He had probably gone to run. He'd get soaked in this downpour.

Sara lay back and listened to the rain. It was soothing and comforting and the perfect background for reliving last night's conversation with Harry.

"I love you, Sara Peters," he had said, and this time she had believed him. This time she had answered him, and she had no doubts about the rightness of that.

She sighed and turned to watch Liza sleep. Oh, there were things they would have to ponder. Nothing had changed about that. They still lived in two different parts of the country, still had had two very diverse lifestyles. There were the children to think of and how best to manage this romance without disrupting their lives.

Sara frowned. L. C. already had shown signs of withdrawal. He had been badly shaken when Harry had gone back to New York, even though Sara had tried to prepare all the children for the fact that Harry was simply a guest, not a permanent member of the family. Still, L. C. had idolized Harry, basking in the glow of his attentions and obvious fondness for the youngster.

The door banged back against the wall as Harry came into the room. Liza jumped and woke with a start.

"Harry, you're all wet," she observed sleepily.

"Decided to take my shower outside this morning," Harry noted as he grabbed a towel from the bathroom and started to dry himself.

Sara glanced over to L. C.'s bed. Normally Harry's humor would have at least elicited a smile, if not a full-blown giggle. But the lump had not moved.

Suddenly Sara felt panic. In one move she was on the other bed, pulling back the covers. "Where's L. C.?"

Harry and Liza looked at each other and then back at the pillow Sara had uncovered.

"Oh, my God," Sara whispered and grabbed the phone.

"Maybe he's just out exploring the neighborhood," Harry said hopefully. "You know, trying to scare you."

"L. C. wouldn't do that." She spoke into the phone then, describing the missing boy to the person on the other end, asking that police be called, other guests be questioned.

"He's missing," she told the person on the other end of the phone with a barely contained patience. "I don't need to wait twenty-four hours to know that. He's lost or he's run away, but he's gone and we're going to start ooking for him now. Do you understand that? Not in an hour; not this afternoon; not tomorrow. Now!'' And with hat she hung up the phone.

Immediately she picked it up again and dialed. Harry and Liza stood by, speechless and waiting.

"Odessa? Sara. L. C. has run away. . . . Well, I think I misjudged how upset he was. . . . Yeah. . . . Okay. . . . Thanks.'' She hung up and turned to Harry. "Odessa will be here within the hour. She's bringing D. J., Jefferson, Maella, and some folks from her church to help us. Let's get dressed.''

Harry glanced toward Liza who had taken a position huddled against the headboard of the bed, one fist pressed against her mouth, her eyes wide and brimming.

"Oh, honey, I'm sorry.'' Sara moved to pick her up. "It's going to be all right. We'll find L. C.''

Now the tears came. "Why did he run away?''

Sara's own eyes filled. "I'm not sure, baby. But it'll be okay. I promise. We'll find him and then we'll make it okay.'' She turned the little girl so that they were facing. "Now listen. I need you to be my best helper.''

Liza nodded solemnly.

"When Odessa gets here, you and Maella are going to stay right here in case L. C. calls us on the telephone, okay?''

Liza nodded again.

While they were talking, Harry had gotten dressed. "Why don't you get dressed. Liza and I will stay here by the phone,'' he said.

For a moment Sara just sat there frozen, as if in shock, as the magnitude of L. C.'s disappearance washed over her.

"We'll find him,'' Harry said softly and gave her a hug. "I promise.''

Within the hour, Odessa and D. J. established a command post in the motel room while Maella prepared to keep an eye on Liza. Their neighbors and fellow church members came in droves to join in the search. Jefferson's classmates also came, their young faces serious as they took copies of the xeroxed photograph and description Harry and the manager of the motel had put together.

Harry was worried about Sara. She looked as if she had been up for days. Her face was lined with the anxiety that comes with contemplating the unknown. On two occasions she had excused herself and gone into the bathroom. When she had returned her eyes were red-rimmed and her face splotched with the results of her crying. But the face she presented to the others was quiet and determined. "We'll find him," she said again and again.

"I think you and I should go out together," Harry told her when they were choosing teams for the search.

"No. We should each go separately. We know him, and a lot of the others only have the picture to go on. We can cover twice the distance."

But Harry was resolute. "I want to be with you. I want you with me. I want us to find him together." He understood the depth of her agony when she did not argue the point further but simply nodded.

"We're going now, Odessa," Sara said. "We're going to head toward the beach. "We'll call you every fifteen minutes."

Odessa nodded. "If you get a busy signal, try again. I'll keep the line as open as I can."

"Mama." It was Liza and her voice was a frightened whimper.

Sara scooped her up and held her close. "It'll be okay, Liza. We're going to find L. C., and then we'll all be together again."

"Promise?"

Harry took the child from Sara and hugged her. "We both promise. Now you be a good girl and help Aunt Odessa, okay?"

Liza nodded solemnly, her eyes brimming and her lower lip quivering.

Sara knelt next to where Liza sat. "What do you think L. C. would like for a celebration when we find him?"

The lip stilled. "You mean a party?"

"Well, of course, a party." Sara laughed and ruffled Liza's hair. "Do you think you might be able to plan a party while Harry and I go find L. C.?"

"Can we have ice cream?" All traces of tears had disappeared.

"Of course, we can have ice cream," Sara said.

"We can have triple hot fudge sundaes," Harry added. "We can have the most humongous banana splits you've ever seen with ten scoops of ice cream and three bananas on each one."

Liza was giggling now. "Oh, Harry," she crowed.

"Now you check with Maella over there. I'll bet she knows just where to get the best ice cream sundaes in Charleston." Sara nodded toward Jefferson's mother who took her cue and came to sit with Liza.

"Y'all better get started," she said quietly.

Sara nodded, gave Liza one last hug, and headed for the door.

"We'll call you from the beach area," Harry said to Odessa as he followed Sara to the car.

They parked near a hot dog vendor's stand. For a moment Sara just stood rooted, her eyes judging the magnitude of the task before them. The area looked endless, and there weren't a lot of people around. The rain had stopped, but it had driven everyone inside or off to other pursuits for the time being.

Harry put his arms around her and turned her to face him. "Now listen to me. We're going to find him, and he's going to be fine. We just have to get started."

Sara nodded but did not move. "I'm so glad you're here," she said, her voice breaking.

Harry hugged her tight and heard her whisper, "I'm so scared, Harry."

"Come on," he said, figuring action was the best remedy for their mutual apprehension.

FOURTEEN

The second vendor thought he recognized L. C. "Yeah. He was here real early . . . right after I opened up. Said his dad was waiting for him. You his dad?" He peered at Harry with disapproval, as if Harry were responsible for the loss of this small boy.

"He doesn't have a dad," Sara said. "He lives with me." Then realizing she was getting into too many details she added, "Which way did he go?"

"Hey, lady, I run a business—got customers to tend to. I didn't see the kid leave . . . figured he went back over there where he said his dad was waiting." He glared at Harry one more time.

They checked in with Odessa who was excited to hear that someone had recognized him so quickly. "That's good news," she said. "It means you're on the right trail."

But the trail quickly went cold. They talked to everyone they could, but no one seemed to have seen L. C. except the vendor.

"And that was hours ago," Sara lamented as they trudged along. "He could be anywhere. What if he got a ride? He could be miles from here. What if—"

"Stop it, Sara," Harry ordered. Then more calmly he added, "We'll just finish this area and then move on. You can't give up."

"Let's call Odessa."

But Odessa had heard nothing more, and it was with heavy hearts and no conversation that Sara and Harry proceeded down the beach.

"Let's check in here," Harry said indicating a small restaurant close to the road.

No one had seen L. C., but the manager agreed to post a copy of the picture and description and call if he had any news.

"Why don't you folks have a cup of coffee before you go on," he said kindly. "Pardon me, ma'am, but you look all done in."

Sara smiled. "Thank you. Coffee would be nice."

The waitress brought coffee, juice, and homemade muffins to the booth where they had settled. It was near the window so Sara could keep watch.

"Tell me what you meant when you told Odessa that he must have been more upset than you thought?"

Sara glanced at Harry and then went back to scanning the surrounding area for any sight of L. C. "It's nothing," she muttered.

"It's more than nothing, Sara. I'm not blind or completely insensitive. You think I didn't notice L. C.'s coolness towards me since I arrived?"

"He's a little boy, Harry. Some things are hard for him to understand, especially given what he's already had to deal with in his short life."

"You mean his family's abandoning him?"

Sara nodded. "That, coupled with the fact they've made no effort to contact or come back for him. For a long time he believed that would happen you know. He used to tell me how they'd send for him as soon as his daddy got a job. He'd explain in the most adult terms how hard things were financially for the family and how his stepfather was working to take care of all of them, even him, even though he wasn't even his real son. It broke my heart.''

"So, where is his real father?"

"Diane—you remember, the social worker—and I tried to find him. After a while L. C. gave up on his mom and stepfather ever coming, and then he fixed on his real dad. This man would come. But he can't.''

"Why not?"

"Because he died in a car accident two years ago."

Harry frowned.

"And then there was the business of not being adopt- able," Sara continued as if having started she needed to tell it all. "L. C. pretended to be very tough and not at all interested in the idea that a real family might want him, but it hurt all the same. A few times people came out to see about maybe taking Liza. L. C. would go into these moods and then close himself off, become sullen and angry.''

"But no one took Liza either."

Sara smiled. "And that was wonderful news to L. C. He would welcome her home with open arms, play dolls with her—he hates playing dolls—and tell her how it was okay because we were her family, him and me.''

Harry buttered another muffin. The waitress refilled their coffee cups.

"So what happened when Jefferson came along?"

Sara smiled. "He was both scared to death of Jefferson and in complete awe of him. He absolutely idolized that boy.''

"So when Jefferson left . . ."

Sara nodded. "It was awful for him. It was as if he was being left again.''

She took a minute to sip her coffee and eat a piece of muffin. Then she glanced at him and added, "It was the same when you left, you know.''

"He thought I was leaving him?" Harry was astounded. It had never occurred to him that he might have had such an impact on any of the children. "I mean I knew the kids liked me . . ."

"These are not ordinary kids, Harry. They have insecurities that most kids don't have, insecurities about not being loved or worthy of love."

"He thought I dumped him?"

Sara smiled at the choice of words. "Well, not just him. All of us."

"And Liza . . . did she think I left because of her?"

Sara shrugged. "Who knows what Liza thinks most of the time? She's a tough little girl, very resilient. But I suspect that, yes, she felt a bit . . ."

"Abandoned?"

Sara shrugged again. "It's a word they have more than a nodding acquaintance with."

Harry drank his coffee and looked out the window. He seemed completely miserable. "But I came back," he offered after a moment.

"Look, I'm just guessing at best, but L. C. may have been just getting over your leaving and then here you are back. Maybe this time . . ." She stopped because she could not believe the thought that was about to be expressed.

"This time, what?"

"Maybe this time L. C. decided to be the one who did the leaving," she said quietly. Then immediately she took his hand. "Harry, they're children. It isn't your fault. If anything I should have seen this coming."

Harry was quiet for some time. Then with a sigh he said, "Let's get going."

"I'll call Odessa," Sara said, sensing that maybe he needed a moment to himself before they headed out again.

She had just finished talking to Odessa from the pay phone near the door when the woman came in. Clearly she was a regular in the place judging by the way everyone greeted her. Sara was thinking how she wished L. C. had hitched up with someone like this lady when the woman announced, "I know this kid."

Immediately she was surrounded . . . Harry, Sara. the manager, the waitress.

"Well, give me some room, people." She studied the photo for a long moment. "Yep. That's the kid. Said he had to go to the bathroom. Told me his Mom was waiting and had sent him in search of one." She frowned at Sara. "He ran away, huh?"

"Did you see which way he went?" Harry pulled out the rough map of the area the motel manager had given him and offered it to the older woman.

"Yep." She studied the map. "He used this bathroom here at the campgrounds. Stayed in there a right smart time. That's what had me suspicious. Seemed to me that since he took so long to find a bathroom and then he stayed in there so long, his mom would come looking. But I didn't see no sign of her . . . you." She glanced at Sara.

"Did you see where he went when he came out of the bathroom?" Sara asked.

"Headed this way." She indicated an area not too far from the restaurant.

"Did you follow him?"

The lady became defensive at that. "The storm hit. I had to find shelter myself. Besides how was I to know . . ."

"It's okay," Sara said soothingly. "Thank you so much for your help. Thank you all." She included the restaurant manager and waitress.

"Let's go," Harry said and held the door for her.

Almost at a run, they headed in the direction the old woman had shown them. As they came closer to the area, Sara's excitement turned to fear.

It was a part of the beach where businesses had fallen on hard times. There were abandoned and dilapidated buildings and boarded up shacks that had once been vending stands. It was an isolated area, reminding her of a waterfront warehouse district. They passed one building where a vagrant was sleeping in the doorway and another where two boys started to run at their approach.

By the time L. C. had worked up the nerve to find shelter in the dark and forbidding shed, he was soaked. He was sure this was the hardest rainfall he'd ever seen and wondered for a moment if this might be a hurricane. They had studied hurricanes at school, and he knew wind and rain were big parts of such storms.

He huddled just inside the doorway of the shed, wedging himself between the door that swung on one rusted hinge and the sacks marked "sand" piled to the ceiling of the narrow shack. For a while he watched everybody run for cover, but when everyone was gone he felt frightened and alone.

He was also tired. He'd been up most of the night, kept awake by the combination of being in the strange place and the overheard snatches of conversation from Mama and Harry. Then he had been wide awake, planning his move, waiting for dawn so he could go.

He was also hungry. He had no idea how long it had been since he'd bought the pretzel and soda, but his stomach told him it was past mealtime.

The shack was dank and musty, and in his wet clothing he felt cold. He shivered and curled himself tighter against the sacks, resting his head on one of them like a pillow.

When he woke the sun was out again, and there was no sign that it had rained at all. He wondered how long he'd been asleep. He heard voices and saw people back on the beach. Everyone was pretty far from where he was so his movements should arouse no suspicion—if anybody even noticed.

He wondered what Mama was doing, what Harry had said when they'd seen he was gone. He wondered if they'd taken Liza and left by now. And that thought made him start to cry.

"Mama," he whimpered.

"Shh!" Sara commanded. "I hear something."

Both she and Harry froze and listened intently.

Silence.

"I don't hear anything," Harry said.

"Wait. Over this way." And Sara started to move quickly toward the opening of the shed.

"L. C.," she whispered when she saw him, as if to say it louder might make him disappear all over again. "Oh, honey, thank God."

Then she was on her knees, cradling him, rocking him, mixing her tears with his.

"Mama, I'm sorry. Don't go away with Harry, please. I promise I'll be good . . . Liza, too. Please, don't leave us."

The boy was sobbing so hard that his words were only babbling at first, but gradually they sank in. "L. C., I'm not going to leave you. Whatever gave you the idea I would ever leave you or Liza?"

L. C. sniffled and squirmed until he was sitting upright. That's when he saw Harry. "I heard you talking," he said. "You told him you loved him." L. C. jerked his head in the general direction of Harry, but his eyes were angry and accusing.

Sara gave him a bewildered smile. "I do love Harry," she said softly. "That's what happens with grown-ups—if they're lucky."

L. C. moved a little further away. His jaw was set in that stubborn way Sara had come to know so well. "Yeah, I know. When my real mom loved my stepdaddy he said if she loved him, she'd understand that he couldn't take care of me." Now the tough facade crumbled. "He made her leave me." And with that he threw himself back into Sara's arms and started crying all over again.

"Hey, sport, listen." Harry knelt next to them and tried touching L. C.'s shoulder, but the boy pulled himself abruptly away.

"L. C.," Sara said, "I'm going to ask Harry to go and find a telephone, so he can let Odessa and the others know we have found you. Then he is going to get the car so we can go back to the motel and get you cleaned up. And while Harry is doing those things, you and I are going to have a serious talk, young man."

L. C. blinked up at her, realizing for the first time that he might be in more trouble than he thought.

"Do you understand me?"

L. C. sighed and nodded. Having a serious talk with Sara was not something a kid wanted to do on a regular basis.

"I'll be back as soon as I can," Harry said.

"Take your time, Harry. We have a lot to discuss."

L. C. rolled his eyes heavenward and Harry grinned.

"Now then," Sara began positioning herself cross-legged on the ground just outside the doorway. "What is this nonsense about?"

"I dunno," L. C. mumbled, making a great show of working the knot out of one shoelace.

"Well, suppose you start by telling me what you think you heard when you were eavesdropping last night—a habit I might remind you that I put in the same category with tattling and gossiping."

L. C. decided the best defense might be offense. Jefferson had said something about that. "He left before—Harry did—and . . . and he said last night that there were compli . . . complicktions."

"Complicktions?" Sara frowned. "Complications?"

L. C. nodded vigorously. "Yeah, like you being on the farm and him being in New York and . . ." He tried to remember all he had heard. Suddenly, he did and his eyes lit in triumph. "He said *the kids*—he said me and Liza were complic . . . those things."

"So, you figured we grown-ups would just take the easy way out—just up and leave you?"

L. C. nodded.

Sara was frustrated. After everything she'd put into caring for this kid, hadn't he realized that she wasn't like his mother or his stepfather? She sighed.

"L. C., you and Liza are a part of my life. You are my family just like Jefferson is and Tommy Lee is and all the others I've told you about."

"But you let them take Jefferson," he challenged.

"Jefferson found his real family and being with them is right for him. It doesn't mean I love him any less."

"I don't know where my real family is," the boy said with a sniffle.

"Yeah, I know. And sometimes even when we know where that real family is, it isn't the best thing. Do you understand? See, L. C., not everybody who has a child is cut out to be a parent or to have a family. Does that make any sense?"

"You mean my real mom was bad?"

"No, I mean your real mom got into a situation she didn't know how to handle. It's a little like you today. When you started out this morning it probably seemed like you were doing the exact right thing. But I'll bet after a while it got pretty lonely and scary."

L. C. nodded and went back to fixing his shoelace.

"And I'll bet that if Harry and I hadn't found you when we did you might have done something that maybe would turn out to be a mistake."

"You mean like maybe my mom thought she was doing the best thing, but she was really making a mistake?"

"Something like that. But maybe what your mom did wasn't such a terrible thing. Maybe she knew that if you stayed with her, you'd have some hard times . . . with your stepfather." She tried to see his expression but he kept his own head down. "I mean you told me you weren't too happy with him." She saw the tears land.

"He used to hit me."

"Oh, L. C., I'm sorry." She pulled the child onto her lap once again and rocked with him. "You know what I think? I think your mom thought that if she left you at that gas station you'd find a new family and guess what? You did. You found me and Liza and now Jefferson and Ling . . . and Harry."

L. C. stiffened at the mention of Harry's name. "Harry left us."

"But he came back," Sara crooned. "And you know what? Harry came back because he loves us."

"He loves you."

"Oh, well, you see Harry understands that loving me means loving you and Liza and Jefferson. You know, Harry could have gone on vacation to a beautiful island with Nancy and Greg instead of coming down here to see Jefferson. He could have ridden in a big airplane and gone swimming in the ocean and had all sorts of fun like that. But he didn't do that."

"He came with us," L. C. said softly, and Sara knew she was beginning to get through to him. "Jefferson says Harry is a . . . bad dude."

When Sara frowned, L. C. giggled. "That means he's okay. Bad is good, get it?" He punched her playfully.

And suddenly it was over—the hours of tension and fear and frustration. They were a mother and her child frolicking on the beach, giggling and chasing each other to the edge of the surf, dancing just out of reach of the waves and holding hands.

That was the sight that greeted Harry as he parked the car on the side of the road and made his way down the small dunes to where they were.

"Harry's it," Sara called tagging him and running.

He took his cue and went after L. C. "Not for long," he called and was rewarded by the boy's excited giggles. "Gotcha," he shouted as he pulled L. C. down on the soft sand and began to roughhouse with him.

After a moment their laughter died, and they simply looked at each other. "You love Mama," L. C. announced as he squinted up at Harry.

"Yeah, I do. Are you okay with that?"

"Does that mean you're gonna stay for good?"

"Tough question. Would you like that?"

"Yeah."

"And what if I said that might not be possible?"

L. C. frowned. "I don't want you leaving Mama and making her sad. She cried when you went away before."

Harry glanced over his shoulder at Sara.

"You did, too, young man," she said. "Now, both of you get up from there and clean off some of that sand. Odessa is going to be waiting for us."

"Child, you better get over here and give your Aunt Odessa just the biggest hug!"

L. C. grinned and ran to Odessa's waiting arms.

"And don't you ever give me or your Mama such a scare again, young man. You understand me?"

L. C. nodded solemnly, then took his turn being hugged by everyone crammed into the small motel room.

Liza was dancing around the room she was so excited. And Sara and Harry spent several minutes thanking everyone for the long hours of help.

"Party," Liza cried as soon as the first flush of excitement had quieted.

"Absolutely, party," Harry said, scooping Liza up in his arms. "What have you and Maella worked out?"

Maella grinned shyly. "Tell him," she coached.

"We're all going back to Odessa's house, and Maella is going to show you where to buy the ice cream and the bananas and stuff, and we're gonna make those splits."

"Wait a minute," Sara said laughing. "You're going to make Harry pay for the party?"

Liza gave her a look of exasperation. "He's got all the money," she said and everybody laughed.

"Well, you know, I think maybe L. C. should pay for this party. After all, it's because of him that there's a party in the first place."

L. C. looked distinctly uncomfortable.

"He don't have no money," Liza shouted.

"Doesn't have any," Sara corrected automatically, but her focus was on Harry who was now sitting next to L.C., his arm around the boy's shoulders.

"Oh, I think L. C. has enough to cover this. What do you say, L. C.? Will you buy the ice cream?"

L. C. glanced at Harry warily. Sara did not miss the way Harry gave the boy a gentle hug and an encouraging smile.

Then L. C. grinned. "Sure. Let's go."

"Well then," Odessa announced, "everybody back to our house for banana splits."

"You and Liza go on with Odessa," Harry urged Sara as she lingered. "L. C. and I will be along."

"L. C., did you take money from Harry's wallet when you left this morning?" L. C. looked away.

Harry took the boy by the shoulders and turned with him toward the door. "Now, Mama, that's between L. C. and me. We'll work it out." Still, she seemed reluctant to leave them. "Go on. I need the practice. I don't have much experience with this parent thing."

"Okay, here's the deal," Harry declared later that evening when they had all returned to the motel room. "Your mom and I are going to sit out on the balcony for a while. We're going to have a long talk. When we finish talking, which may be tonight and may be tomorrow and may be next week, we'll be having a family meeting to tell you about that talk, okay?"

Both children nodded. They were exhausted, but they fought off sleep because what Harry was saying seemed to be something really major.

"*If,*" Harry continued, "*If* you hear something that is

upsetting or scary to you, you are to ask about it right away, understood?'' Solemn nods from both children. ''*However,* I do not expect you will be hearing anything because your mother has told me how she frowns on eavesdropping, and we wouldn't want to do anything that might displease mother, would we?''

Both dark heads shook gravely from side to side.

''Good. Then we have a deal. Kids in bed asleep. Adults on the balcony doing grown-up talk. Okay? Okay. Now, under the covers.''

Both children scampered for their respective beds. First Harry, then Sara, kissed them goodnight. Harry noticed how Sara hugged L. C. a little longer.

''Goodnight, children,'' he said as he turned out the light.

''Goodnight, Harry,'' they answered in chorus and then giggled.

''My lady,'' he said softly holding open the sliding door to the balcony for her.

''Leave it open a crack so we can hear them if they call,'' she said.

''Yes, Mother,'' Harry teased. ''Now come here and give me a hug. It's been a very long day.''

She came happily into his arms. ''It's hard to believe after the way this day started out that it could end so nicely.''

They stood together, rocking a little to unheard music, and pondering the events of the day.

''You know, Sara, something really important happened to me today.''

''Tell me about it.''

''Actually, it's been happening for some time now. Maybe ever since I fell off that bike in that storm.''

''Does it have to do with hitting your head?'' She smiled at him.

And he grinned back. ''Yeah, I think maybe I finally knocked some sense into myself.'' Then the smile disappeared and he frowned. "Nancy told you about Catherine, didn't she?"

"I would have rather heard it from you."

"Yeah . . . well." He led her to the two porch chairs, and they sat down, facing each other, holding hands. "You know, when Catherine did that—killed herself—the first thing I felt was guilt. I hadn't done enough. I hadn't loved her enough. Something. Then after a while, there was this . . . rage. And it was too awful to even contemplate, so I just kept stuffing it back in, not talking about her or the suicide, not letting anyone see this horrible consuming anger."

Sara was surprised at the bitterness in his voice. She had never heard him talk like this before. She wanted to reach out to him and make it better.

"And finally," he continued, "when I knew I was killing myself with anger as surely as she had killed herself with pills, I lapsed into hurt. And I thought if I didn't trust anyone, if I didn't allow myself to give anything away, to love anyone, well, then I'd never have to feel that kind of pain again."

"Is that why you took the bike trip?"

"Yeah. It seemed perfect . . . just me out there alone with no expectations of myself and no demands from anyone else. And it was going okay, although I was a little unprepared for the sheer loneliness of it." He smiled again, and Sara breathed easier.

"And then?"

Now he laughed the laugh she knew she had come to love in those weeks he had spent with them—low, rumbling, coming from deep inside. How she had missed hearing that. "You know this part," he said. "Don't pretend you don't."

She grinned. "Tell me anyway."

He relaxed in the chair and studied the stars. "Well, let's see, I came to and found myself held prisoner in this madhouse a hundred miles from civilization with this absolutely stark raving lunatic in charge who ran around gathering up lost souls and strays to people her particular kingdom." He leaned forward and whispered seriously, "She cast a spell on me, you know. She does that to everybody."

"Really?"

"Sure. She does something magic and before you know it people are falling in love with her—people who have no intention of ever loving anybody ever again. It's really spooky."

"Sounds terrible."

"Oh, no. That's the weird part. The people who fall in love with her feel absolutely great. Their whole world gets turned around."

"And what happens when they leave the kingdom?"

"Well, now that's the really eerie thing." He glanced around as if checking to see if anyone were listening. Then he whispered, "The magic still works."

"No," Sara whispered back with mock shock.

"In New York City even. I know. It happened. I got out of the kingdom, went home, and you know what?"

Sara giggled but shook her head.

"I couldn't shake it—the magic. I mean I love New York . . . sorry, I know that sounds like a commercial, but I really do. I've been to many places—Europe, China, exotic places—and I always was so glad to get back to New York."

"So, what happened this time?"

"It was crazy," he said, sweeping one hand through his hair in exasperation. "The city is dirty and noisy and there's crime all over the place and there are people in pain there . . . all over the place."

Now she was laughing. "Oh come on, Harry, I've never even been to New York and I know all that. You've lived there all your life."

"I know that up here." He tapped his forehead. "But in here?" He tapped his chest where his heart would be and shook his head. "I missed the farm and the quiet and the walks in the woods, not to mention you and the kids and Ling. Hell, I even missed Amos. Everywhere I went I was having these . . . thoughts."

"Thoughts?"

"Yeah. I'd see someone panhandling, and I'd think about Sara and how she would react. I'd walk down the street and see it from her eyes, not mine. I'd come out of a restaurant and feel guilty for having paid for an expensive meal when the guy on the street was hungry. Do you know what? One night I had a sandwich at the deli, and I couldn't finish it. I figured I'd take the other half for lunch."

She nodded.

"I came out of the deli and there was this guy on the corner—he wasn't begging. He was just there . . . in tattered clothes, looking like he hadn't eaten in a while and . . . I handed him the sandwich."

"That was very nice," Sara noted with a smile.

"Nice? Nice! It was completely out of character. It was the most . . ." He searched for words. ". . . the most completely out of character . . . I mean, it's something my mother would do . . . but . . ."

"Harry, it's okay. Think of it this way. The next time you'll have a better grip on yourself. In the meantime it was a lovely gesture."

"But fruitless, don't you see? I mean what's giving a sandwich to one unemployed street guy going to accomplish in the scheme of things."

"Not much," she agreed. "Of course, for that man on that night in that moment, it was a gesture of possibly miraculous proportions."

"But the point is until I met you I would never have even had the thought to do something like that. You have bewitched me. My God, I think if I'm not careful you'll turn me into a raving liberal."

Sara made a face. "Oh no, not that."

They both laughed and settled back in their chairs. They stayed that way for several minutes, not talking, just enjoying the warm night and each other.

"Sara?"

"M-m-m?" She had closed her eyes, savoring the salt-scented breeze, the feel of her hand in his.

"Let's get married."

Sara was sure she must have misunderstood, but before she could say anything, he turned to her and rushed on. "Come on, what do you say? I know there's a lot of stuff to work out, but we love each other, and today I realized what I had given up when Catherine died. I gave up the possibility of a family. I gave up a dream I had had since I can remember. When I came down here, that dream was dead, but then you came into my life and made me see that it was possible."

She had never felt so incapable of saying so little.

"Married," she managed. It wasn't her nature to be coy. She had certainly dreamed of the possibilities. But the fact that he had considered the idea as well was both staggering and exciting. "Harry, I . . ."

"You want the full treatment? Okay." He moved to kneel on one knee, taking her hand in his. His face was completely serious, his voice low and steady. "Sara Peters, I love you. I want to marry you. I know you love me as well." She started to speak, but he silenced her with a finger on her lips. "Let me finish. I know there's a lot to work out—where we will live, your work, my work, meeting my family. But none of that matters. You've taught me that. It's all possible because we love each other. Together we can make this work. We can adopt Liza and L. C. and be together, on the farm, in New York, wherever. We can make a family. What do you say, Sara?"

It was as if he had read her thoughts over all those weeks since he had gone back to New York. How many times had she thought about why it wouldn't work and how it might? And here he was saying exactly the same thing . . . something that could only happen if they both believed it could.

"Sara?" He was still on his knees, his face a mask of worry. It had never occurred to him that she might turn him down. Ever since the idea of proposing had solidified this evening as they sat in Odessa's living room, the one thing he had never considered was that she might actually say no.

She took his face between her hands and leaned down to kiss him. There were tears on her cheeks. "Oh, Harry," she whispered, "I love you."

"Is that a yes?"

"A definite yes," she agreed.

He grinned then and stood up. "Good, because I don't think my knees are up to this kneeling thing," he said, pulling her into his arms for a kiss that promised many things.

EPILOGUE

Sara woke early. It was a habit born of years of farm living, where rising at dawn was a normal routine. Harry slept soundly. But Sara was always anxious to get out into the city. In the months since she and Harry had married, she never tired of the time they spent in New York.

Of course, neither of them could ever think of leaving the farm forever, but from her first visit Sara had understood the fabled attraction of the city. It was on that first visit that they had decided the best plan would be to spend school time in the city and all summers and holidays at the farm. The plan offered the best of both worlds in that it allowed them to be in North Carolina during Sara's busy art fair season and in New York during the times that were busiest for Harry. The children had been apprehensive at first, but they had adjusted quickly, making friends and getting settled into a routine that now included Harry's parents as beloved grandparents.

As quietly as possible Sara dressed in sweats and running shoes and tiptoed out of the room.

"Good morning," she said to Liza and L. C. who were sitting on the floor in front of the television, eating cereal and watching cartoons.

215

Emma, their housekeeper, smiled. "The coffee's on and there are muffins and juice." She returned to watering the plants.

From that first visit they had established an easy friendship that included Emma's understanding that Sara could not abide being waited on.

"Thanks, Emma," Sara said as she downed a glass of juice. "I'm going to walk. I'll be back in an hour."

On her way out of the building she was greeted by the elevator operator and the doorman, both of whom were now like old friends.

On the street she started to walk toward Fifth Avenue. All her life she had heard about Fifth Avenue, and now she understood what all the fuss was about.

As she strode along she found herself smiling as she passed each landmark. There was the Trump Tower—certainly a controversial newsmaker in the past few years. And then there was Tiffany's—a fortress of white marble. St. Patrick's had a special magic all its own. But, as always, at each corner she was tempted by the intriguing possibilities of each side street. She felt as if she could spend the rest of her life in this city and still never fully discover it.

Finally she gave in and began moving east down one side street to Madison and then back up the next and then down the next all the way to Lexington and back to Fifth and so on. Each block held new treasures. As she walked, the streets filled with people, and she began to play the game she had created on that first morning walk she'd taken . . . how many people could she make smile?

"Good morning," she said as she passed a shopkeeper setting out his wares or a businesswoman waiting for the light. "Hi," she called to the man at the newsstand, and there she got a full-blown grin.

But there was also a side of her walk that was not so pleasant, and increasingly she struggled with her frustration at not being able to make a difference. The homeless street people tugged at her heart. There were so many of them. She passed a man lying in a doorway, pressed up against the iron security gate that covered the entrance.

"Lady," he called, "got a quarter? Just need one more quarter for coffee."

Sara stopped. "I'm so sorry," she said. "I've come out without any money. I'm sorry." After the first week she had stopped carrying money, since she was tempted to fill every outstretched hand and when she ran out of coins she always felt guilty for the ones still empty. No, there had to be a better way.

The man gave a low growl and curled back into his fetal position.

Sara moved on.

She saw people everywhere who were in need. She studied their faces. Many of them were exhausted, beaten, defeated. She passed a cardboard box she had noticed on her way down and which she knew was home to an old woman. The woman sat crosslegged on the sidewalk, sheltered by her box, and ranted at every passing person.

"Government . . . big shots . . . poor old woman . . . land of the free . . ."

Sara was almost back to the apartment and intent on having a serious talk with Harry about getting something going for some of these people when she first saw the child. Boy or girl? There was no way of telling. The child wore short-cropped hair except for a long skinny braided piece at the neck, dirty and ripped jeans, name-brand sneakers that looked new and a t-shirt that said *Party or die*. He or she was rummaging through a trashcan in an alley between Harry's building and its neighbor.

"Hey," Sara called determined to make contact.

The kid gave her the look of a startled deer and ran.

"No, come back," Sara called.

"Are you all right, Mrs. Hixon?" The doorman from their building seemed to have appeared out of nowhere.

"I'm fine, Ralph. I just saw this child looking through the trash. I thought perhaps . . ."

Ralph glanced toward the alley. "That's nothing for you to be concerned about," he said tersely, glaring down the alley for any further sign of the urchin. "The kid hangs around here sometimes. I'm sorry if he bothered you."

"He didn't bother me, Ralph. I think he must need some help. Do you know who he is or who his parents are?"

The doorman looked at her as if she were speaking a foreign language. Then he gently ushered her toward the entrance to the large building where they lived. "He doesn't have a name. We just call him *Kid*. Sometimes we let him do odd jobs, but most of the time he's a pest. You'll want to be careful before you get involved with these street kids, Mrs. Hixon," he warned.

"Everyone has a name," Sara retorted as she stepped into the elegant lobby that stood in sharp contrast to the alley she'd just left.

"Yes, ma'am," Ralph replied as he rang for the elevator. He started to return to his post and then turned, "Ma'am, excuse me, but the city is different from . . . other places. Emma has told us about the work you do for the children down in North Carolina, but things are different here."

"Children are children, Ralph," she replied softly just as the elevator doors closed.

Everybody was concerned about her. What about these people who were living on the streets? What about a child rummaging through garbage to find his next meal?

"Harry, we have to find this child," she said the moment she walked through the door. "The one who hangs around in the alley next to your building. Ralph tells me the *kid*—as he calls him—is just somebody who lives on the streets and hangs out here sometimes. But, Harry, this is a child . . . a child who was rummaging through a garbage can when I saw him, a child who looked as if I had just threatened him when I called to him.''

Harry shook his head, smiling. He should have known. Given Sara's history with runaways, strays, and orphans, it was not surprising that sooner or later she would find a child who needed her in New York.

"Come out on the terrace with me, Sara." She followed because she was still expecting an answer, expecting to devise a plan for making contact with the child in the alley. Instead he offered her juice.

"Harry, you don't understand. We need to move on this. Now, do you know this child or not?"

She was pacing the length of the terrace.

"I've seen him around," he admitted uncomfortably.

"And?"

He walked to the railing and looked out over the city. "And nothing. Look, honey, in this town there are thousands of people without a place to be at night. Some of them are children. Hell, a lot of them are children. The best we can offer is shelter programs, meal programs, and that sort of thing."

"Harry, this is not some faceless statistic. This is a youngster . . . who apparently makes his home in your alley and takes his meals from your garbage. This boy is someone who is recognized by the people who work and live in this building. If any one of you saw him twenty blocks from here you would know who he was."

"You can't save them all, Sara," he said softly.

"We can try." Her face was set in that stubborn way he had come to recognize would allow no compromise. Then suddenly her expression softened. "Harry, we have to try . . . please."

"You're intent on saving the world aren't you? I mean the weaving thing is just a front, right?"

She grinned then and seemed to relax. She picked up the glass of juice he'd poured for her. She knew she had him. "Now here's what I was thinking we could do. . . ."

Harry sighed and then smiled. "You're absolutely impossible, you know."

She laughed. "Yeah, I know, but admit it, Harry. That's one of the reasons you love me."

"What's going on?" L. C. asked from the doorway.

"Your mother may have found us a new addition for our family."

"Radical," L. C. noted and ran to report to Liza.

Harry pulled Sara to her feet and into his arms. "Totally radical," he said, and just before he kissed her, he whispered, "I love you, Sara."

SHARE THE FUN . . .
SHARE YOUR NEW-FOUND TREASURE!!

You don't want to let your new books out of your sight? That's okay. Your friends can get their own. Order below.

No. 105 SARA'S FAMILY by Ann Justice
Harrison always gets his own way . . . until he meets stubborn Sara.

No. 22 NEVER LET GO by Laura Phillips
Ryan has a big dilemma. Kelly is the answer to *all* his prayers.

No. 23 A PERFECT MATCH by Susan Combs
Ross can keep Emily safe but can he save himself from Emily?

No. 24 REMEMBER MY LOVE by Pamela Macaluso
Will Max ever remember the special love he and Deanna shared?

No. 25 LOVE WITH INTEREST by Darcy Rice
Stephanie & Elliot find $47,000,000 *plus* interest—true love!

No. 26 NEVER A BRIDE by Leanne Banks
The last thing Cassie wanted was a relationship. Joshua had other ideas.

No. 27 GOLDILOCKS by Judy Christenberry
David and Susan join forces and get tangled in their own web.

No. 28 SEASON OF THE HEART by Ann Hammond
Can Lane and Maggie's newfound feelings stand the test of time?

No. 29 FOSTER LOVE by Janis Reams Hudson
Morgan comes home to claim his children but Sarah claims his heart.

No. 30 REMEMBER THE NIGHT by Sally Falcon
Joanna throws caution to the wind. Is Nathan fantasy or reality?

No. 31 WINGS OF LOVE by Linda Windsor
Mac & Kelly soar to new heights of ecstasy. Are they ready?

No. 32 SWEET LAND OF LIBERTY by Ellen Kelly
Brock has a secret and Liberty's freedom could be in serious jeopardy!

No. 33 A TOUCH OF LOVE by Patricia Hagan
Kelly seeks peace and quiet and finds paradise in Mike's arms.

No. 34 NO EASY TASK by Chloe Summers
Hunter is wary when Doone delivers a package that will change his life.

No. 35 DIAMOND ON ICE by Lacey Dancer
Diana could melt even the coldest of hearts. Jason hasn't a chance.

No. 36 DADDY'S GIRL by Janice Kaiser
Slade wants more than Andrea is willing to give. Who wins?

No. 37 ROSES by Caitlin Randall
It's an inside job & K.C. helps Brett find more than the thief!

No. 38 HEARTS COLLIDE by Ann Patrick
Matthew finds big trouble and it's spelled P-a-u-l-a.

No. 39 QUINN'S INHERITANCE by Judi Lind
Gabe and Quinn share an inheritance and find an even greater fortune.

No. 40 CATCH A RISING STAR by Laura Phillips
Justin is seeking fame; Beth helps him find something more important.

No. 41 SPIDER'S WEB by Allie Jordan
Silvia's quiet life explodes when Fletcher shows up on her doorstep.

No. 42 TRUE COLORS by Dixie DuBois
Julian helps Nikki find herself again but will she have room for him?

No. 43 DUET by Patricia Collinge
Adam & Marina fit together like two perfect parts of a puzzle!

No. 44 DEADLY COINCIDENCE by Denise Richards
J.D.'s instincts tell him he's not wrong; Laurie's heart says trust him.

Meteor Publishing Corporation
Dept. 992, P. O. Box 41820, Philadelphia, PA 19101-9828

Please send the books I've indicated below. Check or money order (U.S. Dollars only)—no cash, stamps or C.O.D.s (PA residents, add 6% sales tax). I am enclosing $2.95 plus 75¢ handling fee for *each* book ordered.

Total Amount Enclosed: $_____.

____ No.105	____ No. 27	____ No. 33	____ No. 39
____ No. 22	____ No. 28	____ No. 34	____ No. 40
____ No. 23	____ No. 29	____ No. 35	____ No. 41
____ No. 24	____ No. 30	____ No. 36	____ No. 42
____ No. 25	____ No. 31	____ No. 37	____ No. 43
____ No. 26	____ No. 32	____ No. 38	____ No. 44

Please Print:
Name _____
Address _____ Apt. No. _____
City/State _____ Zip _____

Allow four to six weeks for delivery. Quantities limited.